D1111424

SIX
INNINGS

SIX INNINGS

JAMES PRELLER

SQUARE
FISH

FEIWEL AND FRIENDS
NEW YORK

SQUARE
FISH

An Imprint of Macmillan

SIX INNINGS. Copyright © 2008 by James Preller. All rights
reserved. Printed in the United States of America by
R. R. Donnelley & Sons Company, Harrisonburg, Virginia.
For information, address Square Fish, 175 Fifth Avenue,
New York, NY 10010.

Square Fish and the Square Fish logo are trademarks of Macmillan and
are used by Feiwel and Friends under license from Macmillan.

Library of Congress Cataloging-in-Publication Data
Preller, James.
Six innings : a game in the life / James Preller.
p. cm.
Summary: Earl Grubb's Pool Supplies plays Northeast Gas & Electric
in the Little League championship game, while Sam, who has cancer
and is in a wheelchair, has to call the play-by-play instead of
participating in the game.
ISBN 978-0-312-60240-6
[1. Little League baseball—Fiction. 2. Baseball—Fiction.
3. Cancer—Fiction.] I. Title.
PZ7.P915Si 2008   [Fic]—dc22   2007032846

Originally published in the United States by Feiwel and Friends
Square Fish logo designed by Filomena Tuosto
Book design by Amanda Dewey
First Square Fish Edition: March 2010
3 5 7 9 10 8 6 4
mackids.com

AR: 4.5 / F&P: T / LEXILE: 690L

In memory
of D. Craig Walker,
loyal friend.

—J.P.

A life is not important except in the impact it has on other lives.

—JACKIE ROBINSON

Pregame

Sam Reiser's bed was pushed against a second-floor window that overlooked a stand of cherry trees. The trees on this June morning were filled with birds, chirping like lunatic alarm clocks.

Sam's first thought: *Shut up, birds. I'm trying to sleep.* Second thought: *Big game today.* The championship game. Earl Grubb's Pool Supplies vs. Northeast Gas & Electric. *Jeez,* Sam thought, *couldn't they give better names to these Little League teams? Why didn't they have real names, like the Cubs or the Pirates?*

Three weeks short of thirteen, Sam had already played on teams called Adirondack Wood Floors, Huck Finn's Warehouse, and Dahlia's Dance Studio—with turquoise-trimmed jerseys, no less. That was about as uncool as you could get.

But once the games started, Sam conceded, the names didn't matter. It would take more than a bad name to ruin a good thing like baseball.

Sam wasn't playing in today's championship game, but he would be the announcer. That had become his thing this difficult season; he was the boy in the booth, the voice in the sky, and no one dared say "boo" to him. The digital clock read 6:37. Sam had to pee. That's why he awoke, he guessed, pressure on the bladder; that, or the lousy birds who wouldn't shut up about the brand-new day. The sun comes up, like it does every day, and those featherheads act like it's the most amazing thing in the world.

Chirp, chirp, chirp.

Big wow.

There was a buzzer rigged to Sam's headboard, one of his dad's proud contraptions, designed to make life a little easier. Just push the button and a bell sounded in three rooms of the house. Then his mother or father would come bounding into the room: "Are you all right? How can we help?!" And if Sam didn't look into their eyes—didn't really look—then it would be okay.

Sam made it a point not to look in anyone's eyes.

He decided to wait until at least 7:00. He could hold out that long. Sam passed the time by thinking about baseball. It wasn't exactly a *choice*, like an essay topic selected for a seventh-grade English paper. Sam never "decided" to think about baseball, just as he never "decided" to have black hair. He awoke and baseball was there, a hanging curveball in his consciousness, white leather wrapped around a cushioned cork core, hovering in the center of his mind. Baseball was always there.

He wondered about last night's scores. Who won the Mets-Phillies game? He fretted the results, hungry for details. It was 6:49. Eleven more minutes. Then it would be time. But not yet. Sam lay perfectly still. Body unmoving. A dull ache in the one leg, just above the knee. Still, not so bad today. And like Mike Tyree said, "Not bad is pretty good." Sam understood what Mike meant. It was all how you looked at things, more than "the thing" itself. But then again, it was easy for Mike to say. He didn't know. No one knew how Sam felt.

Thoughts were like a long chain, connected link by link, and as a habit Sam traced them back in his mind, tracking how one thought led to another. He went from birds to baseball to buzzers. But now Sam was thinking about his best friend, Mike Tyree.

Lately things between them had tilted off-balance, like a ship listing starboard, the ballast unstable. They'd talk at the wrong times, or stay silent when someone needed to speak. Their friendship had been strained and stretched in new directions, a bubble about to burst. Take today's game, for example. Sam knew that Mike was thrilled to be playing in it. A true friend, a *best* friend, would be happy for Mike. But Sam didn't feel that way anymore. Things had changed. Sam wasn't glad. Not for Mike, not for anybody. And Sam hated himself for harboring those mean feelings.

Now Sam really had to go. Five more minutes, four more

minutes. He thought about the game. It was going to be a great pitching matchup. Nick Clemente was throwing for Northeast. Clemente was a big kid, the hardest thrower in the league. When Clemente was locked in, he was unhittable, his fastball electric. Sam admired Nick Clemente, the athlete, but he wasn't crazy about him as a person. Clemente was the type of kid who strutted around like he was king of the cafeteria. Big and loud. Nasty, too. But that only made it worse. Because for a pitcher, being mean was an advantage; it gave you an edge. Clemente could throw a baseball through your ear. A batter could never feel too comfortable with Nick Clemente on the mound. Advantage, Clemente.

For the Pool Supplies team, it would be Dylan Van Zant on the bump. Dylan didn't throw as hard as Clemente. He wasn't as impressive. But Dylan was smart, he had a good idea of what to do on the mound, and he had pitched well all season. Dylan didn't strike out many guys, but he was backed by a strong defense, led by shortstop Carter Harris.

Sam stared at the digital clock, waiting. In a split second, three numbers tumbled: six became seven, while five and nine flipped to zeros. Seven o'clock. Sam grabbed the buzzer and squeezed.

It was going to be a great game.

The Game

Earl Grubb's Pool Supplies

PLAYERS	Pos.
Dylan Van Zant	P
Nando Sanchez	3B
Branden Reid	C
Carter Harris	SS
Eamon Sweeney	LF
Scooter Wells	CF
Max Young	2B
Mike Tyree	RF
Alex Lionni	1B
Tyler Weinberg	SUB
Patrick Wong	SUB
Colin Sweeney	SUB

MANAGER: Jeff Reid

ASST. COACH: Andy Van Zant

SCOREKEEPER: Casper Lionni

SPECIAL RULES

1. Each player must play a minimum of four innings in the field.

• HOME •

Northeast Gas & Electric

PLAYERS	Pos.
Justin Pinkney	SS
Frank Ausanio	CF
Angel Tatis	3B
Nick Clemente	P
Steven Smith	1B
Owen Finkel	LF
Travis Green	C
Joey Crocker	RF
Billy Thompson	2B

Luther Dross	SUB
Marty Carbinowski	SUB
Jasper Mednick	ABSENT

MANAGER: Rocco Clemente
ASST. COACH: Ted Pinkney

2. Each player must have a minimum of one plate appearance.
3. All substitutions must be made after the completion of the second and fourth innings.

Top of the First

	1	2	3	4	5	6	R	H	E
VISITORS	-								
HOME									

The one o'clock championship game is almost upon them, like a locomotive approaching from a great distance. The closer it gets, the larger it looms. And now here it is—that big train coming through.

The boys have already taken batting practice. They've warmed up and cooled down; chatted, joked, and poked, until, moments before the first pitch, they grow idle and contemplative.

Coach Reid brings the Earl Grubb's team together for a pregame talk. A muted shout breaks the quiet, hand claps and cheers erupt from inside the dugout. "Team!" they cry.

Up in the announcer's booth, Sam Reiser informs the crowd:

Both teams hustle to the base paths, straddling the white lines that run from home plate to the respective foul poles. They take off their hats, hands on their hearts—Tyler Weinberg has to be reminded, and is, with a friendly whack on the head from Colin Sweeney—and they watch as the flag waves in a soft breeze. The anthem plays on a crackly sound system. And now at last, it's time for the game. Northeast Gas & Electric, the home team by virtue of a superior regular-season record, takes the field.

Dylan Van Zant stands about ten feet from home plate, timing his swing to Nick Clemente's warm-up pitches. Clemente throws nothing but fastballs that explode in catcher Travis Green's glove. *Pop, pop, pop.*

"Balls in!" Green cries out.

The fielders toss their practice baseballs in lazy arcs toward the home-team dugout along the first-base line.

"Coming down!" Green hollers.

The smooth, dark-skinned shortstop, Justin Pinkney, glides over to second base, backed up by the pint-size second baseman, Billy Thompson. Clemente snaps off a half-hearted curveball that floats in like a helicopter. Green snares it deftly, rises, and fires a laser to second base. *Strong arm,* Dylan notes admiringly, *great catcher.*

The umpire, bulky and dressed in dark blue, calls, "Come on. Play ball!"

From his seat in the announcer's booth, behind and above

10

home plate, Sam Reiser feels his heartbeat quicken. *Play ball.*
He leans into the microphone and pushes the black button.

**Leading off for Earl Grubb's Pool Supplies, today's
starting pitcher, Dylan Van Zant....**

As his name is announced, Dylan looks down the third-base line to Mr. Reid, who is stationed in the coach's box. The skipper claps his hands, nods. "Get us started, Dilly."

Dylan has already decided to take the first pitch. It doesn't matter where the ball goes, Dylan won't swing. He wants to see Clemente's fastball, up close and personal. Watch his motion, look for the release point—but mostly, try to relax. Get rid of the bees that are buzzing in his brain. Because here he stands, playing for the championship. How cool is that?

Dylan takes a fastball down the pipe for strike one.

It has begun.

Clemente has the unsettling habit of grunting with each pitch. He's like a bull in a pen, eager to break loose. *Snort, snort, fliiiing.* Already at five feet, ten inches and 170 pounds, Clemente is colossal for a seventh-grader. Scary as all get-go and he knows it. Clemente works quickly. In seconds he's back on the rubber, charging into his delivery; he plays like his hair is on fire.

Dylan swings and misses at a chest-high fastball, corkscrewing his wiry frame into the earth. *Late,* Dylan thinks. *Way late.* He steps out of the box, takes a breath, feels the electric undercurrent from the packed bleachers.

Clemente glowers from the mound, hoofing the dirt with his cleats.

The count is no balls, two strikes. No one out. No runners on base. The game has scarcely begun, but already Clemente has set the tone. He is going to work fast and throw gasoline. His every move an act of defiance, a dare that says, "Hit me if you can."

Down two strikes, Dylan inches his fingers up the bat handle. *Fast to the ball*, he tells himself. Protect the plate. No matter what, don't go down looking. There's nothing worse than striking out with the bat on your shoulders.

Clemente, square-shouldered and built like a soda machine, rocks back into his windup. His hands come together before his chest, pump back over his head, the left knee lifts up as he pivots, pushes off the rubber on a thick right leg, drives toward the plate with maximum force. *Uhhhmmmgh.*

The pitch is just ridiculous. A curve that acts as if it were dropped from the sky. One moment the ball is right there, then it isn't. Gone, vanished, like it fell into a manhole.

Dylan swings and misses. The home-plate umpire signals strike three. Green zips the ball back to Clemente, who sneers with satisfaction.

Batting second, Nando Sanchez. . . .

The name on his birth certificate is Armando, after a grandfather back on the island. Everyone calls him Nando. And he is very fast. Everything Nando does, from eating waffles to fielding grounders, is restless and quick. He swings in short, choppy strokes—a slap hitter, not a power threat. "We will work with that," his father announced one day. "Speed never slumps. Hit the ball on the ground and fly, Nando, fly."

Thin and undersized, Nando bats with an exaggerated crouch, presenting the pitcher with a small strike zone. He takes the first two pitches high for balls. Clemente steps off the mound, angrily slams the ball into his glove. Clemente's fury surprises Nando, almost frightens him. Clemente grunts and fires another pitch.

"Strike one!" the umpire calls.

Hot stuff, thinks Nando, *caliente*. Nando steps out of the box, wipes his lips with the back of his sleeve, tightens his batting gloves, and eyes Coach Reid as he goes through the signs. Reid touches his hat, the indicator, then goes to his belt buckle. Nando understands: *Bunt*. The alert third baseman, Angel Tatis, also seems to sense the possibilities. He creeps in, bent low, his glove licking the tips of the grass.

Nando squares early, showing the bunt, bat held loosely at chest level. The pitch comes in high and tight. Nando falls away, instinctively using his bat for protection. Somehow he manages to bunt the ball foul as he collapses to the ground. Strike two.

"That's okay, Nando! You're okay!" his father shouts from the stands. "Two strikes now, Nando! You've got to protect!" Nando turns to see his father, mother, maternal grandparents, two brothers, and baby sister crowded together in their seats. They have come to watch Nando play in the great champi-

13

onship game. Not watch, no, they've come to cheer—wildly, enthusiastically, passionately. Nando hopes to make them proud on this day, not seeming to realize that it's already been accomplished, long ago. He focuses back on the pitcher.

Clemente stares with reptilian eyes, cold and lifeless. He won't waste a curveball on a weak hitter like Nando. It will be a steady diet of fastballs until Nando proves he can catch up to one.

"You must earn the pitcher's respect," Mr. Sanchez told his son many times. "He has to get *you* out, not the reverse, *comprende*, Nando? That's why you must have confidence. Go to the plate like you own it, like you own the whole field. Swing the bat and make him respect you!"

Nando doesn't stand a chance. Strike three cuts the outside corner, or at least that's how the umpire sees it, and his is the only opinion that matters. It's not a debate club. To Sam's eyes, the ball looked six inches wide of the plate. Tough break for Nando. The first blown call of the day. It wouldn't be the last.

In the Pool Supplies dugout, all the players push forward at once, eager to watch this next matchup. Branden Reid might be the team's hottest hitter, sturdy and broad-shouldered. More than that, he has become one of the leaders of the team, the kid everyone respects. If Branden can't hit Clemente, what chance did anyone else have?

A loud, guttural voice calls out, "Let's go, kiiiiiiid!"

Sam instantly recognizes the voice, for it can only be

Mike Tyree. Sam leans forward to get a better look into the Pool Supplies dugout. At that same instant, Mike returns Sam's gaze, as if they were connected by an invisible thread.

It had happened dozens of times before. It was, in fact, how they became friends, back in Mrs. Geller's first-grade class. It took one wordless exchange—right after Aaron Foley threw up during a math lesson. Spectacularly. Gloriously. Voluminously.

Aaron Foley, short and stocky with a squished-in face that reminded Sam of an English bulldog, did more than toss his cookies. No, Aaron *projected* his vomit across the room, spewing his insides as if fired from a cannon, a thunderous blast of wet barf splattering onto the tile floor.

No one spoke. No one moved.

Mrs. Geller at last motioned to Janice Dingum. "Better fetch Joe the janitor. Tell him to bring a mop"—she paused a beat—"and a large bucket."

At that precise moment, Sam glanced up only to catch Mike staring back at him, his face a mixture of mirth and horror, delight and stunned awe. Somehow each boy knew how the other felt, knew it *exactly*. A telepathy that focused on a single word: *Recess*.

Mrs. Geller asked Austin Hayes to escort Aaron to the nurse's office, a request that Austin accepted with reluctance. The teacher then shooed everyone out onto the playground until Joe arrived with that mop.

On the jungle gym, the boys snickered, recounting Foley's

heroic hurl. Extra recess! Good old Aaron Foley! That's how Sam and Mike began their friendship, sealed with a simple exchange, a look across a silent (but foul-smelling) distance.

Mike will try to sneak away to visit Sam later if he gets a chance. It almost feels wrong that he's on the field, while Sam—the better player—is stuck up there. Mike checks the stands and wonders: *Will they come?* His parents miss so many of his games. But this one is different. This time, it means something to Mike.

He remembers that it was late when he got dropped off after the final regular-season game. The NBA playoffs were on television. Mike waited, still in uniform, watching, mildly interested. The station broke for a commercial.

"So? How'd you do?" Mr. Tyree asked.

"We won," Mike answered.

But Mike's father noted, "I asked how did *you* do."

"Pretty good," Mike said. "I walked, stole a base, and scored. I made a nice play at third base. I like playing the in-field."

"No hits?" his father asked.

Mike didn't have an answer for that.

The commercials were finished, the game was back on. The conversation, Mike knew, was nearly over. "We clinched a spot in the championship game," Mike announced. "It's on

Saturday." Mike's head pivoted from his mother to his father. "It would be great if you can, you know, come to the game."

"You know that Saturdays are tough," his mother commented. "We'll see."

Which to Mike's ears meant one thing: If your sister Candace has an AAU basketball game—and doesn't she always?—then you're out of luck. Because there already was a star athlete in the Tyree family. And her name wasn't Mike.

That's two up and two down for Clemente.
Next to the plate, catcher Branden Reid. . . .

Other boys in the dugout pick up Mike's battle cry. "Come on, kiiiiiiiid," they exhort. More calls come from the lively dugout, hoots of encouragement. Branden Reid eyes Clemente as he walks to the plate, cool as a three-bean salad.

He pulls the first pitch foul down the third-base line, forcing his father to leap out of the way. Coach Reid pulls a handkerchief out of his pocket and waves it. "I surrender, I surrender," he comically gestures to the crowd.

The scattered laughter irritates Branden. He likes his dad and everything, but this isn't the time for clowning around.

Up in the booth, Sam pops a peanut M&M into his mouth. He thinks, *Quick bat. Not too many guys can pull Clemente's fastball.* It comes as no consolation that, in fact, Sam himself is one of the few guys with hands fast enough to do it. Sam loves facing fastball pitchers.

Down on the field, Nick Clemente challenges Branden with another fastball, but this time in a better spot. High and inside, right above the crook of the elbow. Branden barely manages to foul it back off the screen.

Down two strikes, Branden still feels confident. He knows he can catch up to the fastball. He feels loose, relaxed. His bad arm doesn't bother him when he swings the bat. It only hurts when he throws. Branden calls time, steps out of the box, if only to mess with Clemente, who snorts with impatience. All Clemente knows is *now, now, now*. He's pent up, eager to kick down walls. So Brandon dawdles, taps his cleats free of imaginary mud, casually picks a piece of sand out of the corner of his eye.

He got Dylan on an 0–2 curveball, Branden figures. He prepares himself for it, thinking, *Weight back, hands back*. But Clemente comes with a fastball, a pea at the knees. Branden's eyes widen, he swings through the pitch. Branden looks back at the catcher's glove in disbelief. He got beat by a fastball. *Damn, just missed it.*

In baseball, scouts refer to the five tools: speed, glove, arm, power, and the ability to hit for average. It is rare for one player to excel in all five areas. Branden Reid, however, possesses a sixth tool, amnesia, the art of forgetting. Baseball is, after all, a game of failure. The only thing that a player can influence is the *next* play, the *next* at-bat. The strikeouts, the errors, the defeats? Ancient history, best forgotten, or at least pushed aside. So Branden hustles back into the dugout, pulls on the catching gear, and steps back into the sun.

2

Bottom of the First

	1	2	3	4	5	6	R	H	E
VISITORS	O						O	O	O
HOME	-								

Okay, boys, take the field," Coach Reid barks enthusiastically. "No walking between the white lines, Eamon. Put some hustle in that muscle."

Nine players from the Earl Grubb's team trot onto the field. Coach Reid means it: No walking. He demands that every player hustle on and off the field. Alex Lionni, playing first today, tosses a practice roller to Max Young at second base. Shortstop Carter Harris chats with Nando Sanchez near the third-base bag, seemingly lighthearted and carefree. The outfielders, from left to right, are Eamon Sweeney, Scooter Wells, and Mike Tyree. Good speed to chase down fly balls. Branden Reid takes his position behind the plate.

There's a small, round hill in the middle of the freshly

mowed lawn, and that's where today's starting pitcher, south-paw Dylan Van Zant, slowly walks. Yes, walks. Pitchers are different; pitchers are special. They are the only players who are *encouraged* to walk between the lines. In baseball, the pitcher is everything. He holds the five-ounce ball in his hands. The game does not commence until he lets it go. Others can only stand and wait, spit between their teeth, flick a pebble. Nothing happens without the pitcher's permission. Once he throws, time itself begins.

Most kids get used to sitting on the bench. They accept it. But for others, it's accompanied by a displaced feeling, more acutely felt when the team plays defense. That's when you were most aware of it, the status of benchwarmer, the outcast, the kid whom the coach decides isn't quite good enough to play the full six innings.

While the team bats, the bench players—or scrubeenies, as Colin Sweeney calls them—feel a part of everything. The guys are all together, rubbing shoulders, joking around, a team. But after three outs, nine guys grab their gloves and run onto the field, leaving three boys behind. And the gray cement dugout begins to resemble a dungeon, a dreary cell they've been sentenced to.

It doesn't bother Colin Sweeney. Actually, nothing much does. Maybe Colin even prefers it, not that he'd say so. No pressure. You can't exactly screw up while eating sunflower seeds. For Colin, well, to be honest, it was boring in the out-field. Nobody to talk to, nothing much going on. You can stand in right field for *days* and the only thing you'll catch is a sunburn on your nose. Come to think of it, Colin ought to show up one day wearing that white stuff on his nose like the lifeguards at the town pool. What's it called? Zinc oxide. That would get a laugh.

Colin is one of two Sweeneys on the team, along with his brother, Eamon. Identical twins, they are opposites in most ways. Colin is a lefty; Eamon is a righty. Colin talks; Eamon listens. Colin jokes; Eamon laughs. Colin likes rap and rock and watching movies; Eamon practices piano and prefers long books. Colin plays for fun, to run with the boys; Eamon plays for . . . well, he's not exactly sure. Probably he just feels at home when he's around Colin. For all of these reasons and more, Coach Van Zant jokingly refers to Eamon, the righty, as "The Right Sweeney." Colin, the lefty, is known as "The Wrong Sweeney."

The team's resident movie-trivia king and nonstop talker, Colin is already holding court with the other two substitute players, Patrick Wong and Tyler Weinberg.

"Okay," says Colin Sweeney. "I'll give you the quote. You name the movie: '*Listen, Lupus, you didn't come into this life just to sit around on a dugout bench, did you? Now get your butt out there and do the best you can!*'"

Patrick answers instantly, "That's easy. *The Bad News Bears.*"

"Correctomundo," Colin replies. "That's from the original, not the remake with Billy Bob Thornton. Bonus question: What was the coach's name?"

A ball of excess energy, Tyler sits with knees jumping, feet jiggling. He glances at Patrick Wong. They have no idea.

21

"Morris Buttermaker," Colin answers. "Here's one for you, Tyler: 'There's no crying in baseball.'"

"*The Sandlot?*" Tyler guesses.

Colin shakes his head.

"*The Rookie?*"

Nope.

"*Field of Dreams?*" Patrick offers.

"Wrong, Wong," Colin replies. "It's *A League of Their Own.*"

"Oh, with Tom Hanks," Tyler says.

"About the girls' team," Patrick notes. "I liked that movie."

Colin pulls a pack of chewing gum from his bat bag. "Quick, first guy who can name three other Tom Hanks movies gets a piece. . . ."

And so it goes, typical baseball chatter, the talk that fills dugouts everywhere, the words that occupy the spaces the game provides, those gaps when nothing much seems to happen. To love baseball, to truly love the game, you've got to enjoy those empty places, the time to think, absorb, and shoot the breeze. A ball, a strike, a grounder to short. The slow rhythm of the game, a game of *accumulation*, of patterns, gathering itself toward the finish, like the first few miles of a marathon, not dramatic except for what it might mean later in the race.

On the mound, Dylan goes through the regular routine of his warm-ups. Today, he senses something new—a fluttery feeling in his stomach. An unsettled, unrooted sensation, like he might lift off the ground at any minute, floating away like a helium-filled balloon. But mostly, Dylan feels the presence of *eyes*. He is aware of being watched, evaluated, judged. The guys on Northeast Gas & Electric gape at him from the dugout. The fans in the stands size him up. That comes with the position. All pitchers have a little bit of rock star in them. They like the spotlight. Usually.

Like most boys his age, Dylan is keenly aware of his father's presence. Assistant Coach Andy Van Zant stands beside Coach Jeff Reid, looking out on the field like all-knowing generals before a skirmish. The men watch Dylan throw; they nod and whisper; Coach Reid says something, Dylan's father laughs.

Dylan steps off the rubber for a moment, collects himself. He has to stop looking around, his head filled with too many thoughts. Time to clear his mind, focus on the glove, execute one pitch at a time. He rears back and puts everything he's got on the final warm-up pitch.

Branden shouts, "Balls in!" At the final toss, Branden draws his arm back to throw down to second, feels something, then reaches for a better idea. He jogs the ball out to the mound.

"I wanted to deliver this personally," Branden explains, handing the baseball to his batterymate. "One's a fastball, two's a curve," Branden says, repeating the signals every self-respecting ballplayer knows by heart. "Keep the ball low, especially the curveball," he advises. "You're living at the knees today, Dill. Nobody can hurt you if you keep the ball down there."

Leading off for Northern Gas and Electric, shortstop Justin Pinkney. . . .

At the sound of Sam's voice over the loudspeaker, Branden heads back to home plate. "Hey," Dylan calls after him in an urgent whisper. "You nervous?"

Branden smiles and lies through his neat white teeth. "Are you kidding? Look around. This is awesome. What is there to be nervous about?"

And then, impressively, Branden manages to summon up a long, odorous burp followed by a satisfied smirk. Some catchers just have a knack for saying and doing the right thing. Dylan shakes his head, laughing soundlessly. "Get out of here," he says. "Go squat in the dirt where you belong."

At first base, Alex Lionni watches the batter with dreamy interest. To Alex, Justin Pinkney represents more than the leadoff hitter. He is a neighbor, a friend, and a rival. The kid who does everything a little bit better than Alex. But no matter how good Justin got over the years—no matter how much farther he hit the ball, or faster he threw it—Alex's belief in himself was unshaken. Sure, Justin was a nice player all right. But Alex? He was going to be a big-leaguer. He knew it. No matter what his father said.

"You've got to stop dreaming about baseball," Mr. Lionni

had lectured Alex one evening. "Your future is in the classroom, not on the baseball field. Be realistic, Alex. You will never play for the New York Yankees."

Alex stood there, hands dangling at his sides.

"Think about the odds," his father had reasoned. "There are six hundred players in the majors. These players come from all over the United States, and from other countries such as Japan, the Dominican Republic, Argentina, Cuba— all over the world." Mr. Casper Lionni paused, then continued. "Look around, Alex. You are not even the best player on our street."

Alex had nodded absently, licked his lower lip. He knew his father was thinking about Justin Pinkney, three houses down. Alex noted that his father had a smudge of butter on his chin. It glistened in the lamplight, shimmering. Alex watched it curiously, vaguely repulsed.

Alex breathed in and out. He felt the air enter his nose, curl around his stomach, then pass out through his lips. In and out. Just breathe. Father has a shiny chin, shiny chin. Chinny-chinny-chin-chin! Not by the hair on my . . .

"Be practical, Alex," his father pleaded. "I'm sorry, but you were not born into an athletic family. We are scholars, readers, thinkers. Look at me, Alex. I am five feet, six inches tall. I weigh one hundred and fifty-five pounds. To make a success of myself, I had to hit the books, not baseballs."

"I'm tall," Alex reasoned.

"For now," Mr. Lionni said. "I was tall at a young age, too, then I stopped growing."

"You never know," Alex pointed out.

Mr. Lionni looked at his son searchingly. "Alex, do you understand me? Sports are fun. A nice way to spend an afternoon. But schoolwork is more important."

Alex nodded.

He understood.

Oh, he was going to play for the Yankees all right.

He just wasn't going to get any help from his old man.

Alex's neighborhood nemesis, Justin Pinkney, swings at the first pitch, a fastball down the pipe. He smacks a sharp grounder two steps to the right of Max Young at second base. The ball bounces chest high, a charity hop. Max shuffles over, gathers the ball, and makes the easy throw to Alex at first.

Coach Reid calls out, "Very nice, Max. Great job!"

One pitch, one away. Here comes Frank Ausanio, batting second for the home team. . . .

Branden sees that Ausanio appears a little skittish, probably overeager, so he puts down two fingers: curveball. Dylan nods and floats one, up and in, for a ball. The curve doesn't bend at all, just spins. A terrible pitch. Branden frowns, considers his options, and signals for another curve. To win, he figures, Dylan needs to get that pitch working. Dylan isn't Nick Clemente, he can't throw fastballs all day. Nope, he'll have to mix it up, change speeds, hit his spots. "No time like the present," Branden whispers to himself, echoing a favorite phrase of his father's.

The chorus of voices begins:

"Just throw strikes!" somebody shouts.

"Finish your pitches," Dylan's father advises. "Bury that shoulder, Dill."

"Just catch and throw!" comes a voice from the stands. "Catch and throw."

"Come on, Dill. Come on, Dilly-Dill," a teammate implores.

The southpaw ignores the proffered list of suggestions. He knows that if he listens to these sideline soothsayers, he'll make himself crazy by the second inning. Throw strikes, do this, don't do that. It's all easy to say, not so easy to do. So Dylan rocks back, lifts his right knee high to his chest, and breaks off a beautiful pitch. The ball starts on the outside of the plate, then breaks down and in. Ausanio freezes, off-balance. Unfortunately, the curveball is almost *too* good. It seems to fool the umpire, who calls it a ball. The count moves to 2–0.

Can't walk him, Dylan thinks. Time to break out the fastball.

Ausanio, a stocky kid with good power, is sitting on it. He swings hard and drives a grounder down the third-base line. Frank Ausanio—no longer a batter, he is a base runner now, and a daredevil—takes a wide turn around first, thinking double. Eamon Sweeney scurries to the ball with fast, lizardlike steps. He quickly dumps it off to shortstop Carter Harris, positioned as the relay man between the ball and second base. It is a lesson that Eamon has been taught all season long: "Get the ball to Carter."

Carter holds the ball high, cocked behind his ear, daring Ausanio to try for second base. That seems to dissuade the base runner. Ausanio returns to the bag, loudly high-fiving the first-base coach, teammate Marty Carbinowski.

Cheers and yelps come from the Gas & Electric bench: "Waydahgo, waaaydahgo, waaaydahgo!"

Well, folks, there goes Van Zant's no-hitter. Now up, third baseman Angel Tatis. . . .

The first pitch to Angel is intended to be low and away. Dylan badly misfires and the ball skips off Branden's glove to the backstop. In one motion, Branden flings off his mask and scrambles to his feet. He finds the ball as it careens off the screen. Branden barehands it—"He's going!" voices cry. "Throw 'em out!" others implore—and Branden rifles the ball toward second base.

A searing pain shoots through his arm like an electric current, running from his shoulder down to his fingers. The ball, way off-line, bounds into center field. Scooter Wells charges the ball and gloves it before the dust clears around Ausanio's helmet.

Up in the booth, Sam Reiser sees that something is wrong. He knows what it is, too, because he was there when it happened. Branden hurt his arm a few days ago, when Mike,

Sam, and a few others were goofing around on the Sweeneys' trampoline. Sam was sitting off to the side, watching as the boys played "kill the carrier," a roughneck game that basically involved pulverizing each other. Unfortunately, Branden emerged from one pileup clutching his arm.

"You promise not to tell my dad?" Branden demanded. One by one, his friends fell in line. If Branden's father knew about the injury, he would never let Branden play in the championship game. So Branden's secret was safe. Until it came to Mike.

"I can't promise," Mike said. "You should check it out with a doctor, Branden. It might be serious."

Branden scoffed.

Mike looked to Sam for support. Sam looked away, unwilling to get in the middle of it. Mike held his ground. "A doctor should look at it," he insisted.

Branden stared hard at Mike, then looked to Sam. "Okay," Branden relented. "Tell you what, my mom is a nurse at St. Mary's. I'll ask her. Is that good enough for you?"

Branden's mother, who likewise reluctantly promised secrecy, gave his arm a careful evaluation. She pronounced Branden fit to play, so long as he was careful.

For a terrible moment, Branden is seeing spots, red and purple dots. He shakes his head, glances around unsteadily, picks up his mask, and pulls it down over his face. He doesn't rub his shoulder or give any sign of discomfort. Instead, he checks his father's reaction with a sideways glance. Then he looks up in the stands at his mom, who returns his gaze. She touches her shoulder. He nods in response. And somehow that makes him feel better. He isn't alone.

Branden blows on his throwing hand, wipes it on his pants. "Ball slipped," he mutters. He squats behind the plate. Branden puts down a hand to steady himself. A weird image pops into his mind—he imagines his right arm lying on the ground, as if it had fallen off completely, like a doll's arm. A few seconds pass; he feels okay. Branden turns his thoughts to the batter, Angel Tatis.

Angel is a good ballplayer, and a fantastic drummer, too. He plays in the middle-school band with Branden. That's how they first got to know each other, since they came from different elementary schools. It is also where Branden learned a little something about Angel Tatis. "I hate to walk," Angel once confided to Branden over the winter. "I mean I really hate it," Angel insisted with genuine loathing. "I'm up at the plate, I'm there to swing the stick."

And like any good catcher, Branden filed that information away in the back of his mind, like an index card alphabetized in a gray metal cabinet. Well, today was the championship game—*No time like the present*, Branden decides.

"Time, blue," Branden requests of the home-plate umpire. He ambles to the mound.

"What's up?" Dylan asks, annoyed by the interruption.

"I know this guy," Branden says, tilting his head toward the batter's box. "Great hitter, but he's a free swinger. Don't throw him a strike. He'll go fishing, trust me."

The count works to 1–2, with Angel hacking at a couple of pitches out of the strike zone. Branden calls for a curveball. The pitch bounces in front of the plate. Like a hockey goalie, Branden splays downward and blocks it. The ball trickles only a few feet away, but Ausanio sprints for third. Branden pounces on the ball and sees that he has Ausanio dead to rights. He hesitates. He pumps once, holds the ball, and watches as Ausanio slides safely into the bag.

"Throw the ball, Branden!" Coach Reid calls out. "You've got to make that play, son!"

Branden looks to his father, nods once. He flips the ball underhand to Dylan. Why hadn't he thrown the ball? Was he worried about the pain that he knew would surely come? No, Branden didn't think so. For the pleasure of throwing a guy out at third, Branden would gladly pierce his ears with a screwdriver. It wasn't the pain that bothered him. Besides, he trusts his mother. She said it was a bruised muscle, it would get better after a week or ten days. The problem, Branden understands, is that he was afraid of throwing the ball into left field. Screwing up and giving a run away. It was too risky. Branden no longer trusted himself; he had no idea where the ball was going. *What good is a catcher who can't throw?* Branden asks himself.

"Play's to first base," Coach Reid barks to the infield.

From his lofty perch, like a bird on a wire, Sam sees and

understands. Coach Reid is willing to give up a run to get the sure out. Any grounder to the infield and the base runner on third will score. Okay, fine. Sam can't argue with the strategy. It is only the first inning. But Sam's gut tells him it's a mistake. Earl Grubb's is facing Nick Clemente, and his stuff today looks filthy. Every bone in Sam's body tells him they can't let Northeast Gas & Electric get on the board first.

Branden sets up behind the plate. The count is 2–2. He holds his glove unusually high, squeezing it open and closed, a signal for Dylan to climb the ladder. "Come on, Angel," Branden mutters to himself. "I know you can't lay off the high hard one." He wants the strikeout. Dylan nods, trusts his catcher completely. Dylan feels the ball in his glove, grips it across the seams, reaches back for something extra, and blows Angel away with a high fastball. Strike three! Yes!

Two outs, runner holds at third. Batting cleanup, big Nick Clemente. . . .

Sam Reiser leans back and savors the moment. He is now completely caught up in the game. Everything else falls away, all life's distractions, like a skin that's been shed. He doesn't worry about his hair, or homework, or doctors. He isn't concerned about tomorrow. That's what baseball gives him, the urgency of the here and now.

Sam watches Nick Clemente approach the plate and has to shake his head, laughing. Every Little League has one, the kid who looks like he's three years older than everybody else.

A giant among boys. Taller, bigger, stronger. Clemente weighs twice as much as most second basemen. He could probably *eat* most second basemen. And if you look closely, right there above the top lip, he's even wearing a scrawny, mouse-colored mustache. This kid *shaves*. Nick Clemente steps to the plate, arrogantly twirling his metal bat like a baton.

Clemente takes the first pitch for a called strike. His opinion differs and Clemente expresses his displeasure to the local authorities. "You're killing me, ump," Clemente grunts under his breath. "That pitch was at my ankles."

Dylan tries the same pitch again, but this time gets it up into the zone. A mistake from the moment it leaves Dylan's fingertips. Clemente offers a hellacious swat.

Dylan's instant thought: *Dinger.*

Out in center field, Scooter Wells knows better. He instantly realizes that the ball is going to stay within the yard. Most important, Scooter figures he's got a chance to catch it. Somehow he does all that figuring—the mathematics of it, the cool calculus of force and trajectory, distance and wind patterns—by pure instinct. It's a gift; he knows how to read a ball coming off a bat. To Scooter, center field is like a fire tower in the high peaks of the Adirondacks, an all-seeing observation post, the ideal vantage point to watch as the game unfolds.

Most times, nothing happens. An outfielder can chill out, relax. Take off his glove and blow into a perspiring palm, gaze around, mentally rehearse skateboarding tricks, then return his attention to the game. Sometimes Scooter would worry that he'd forget. Get lost in daydreams only to awaken to shouts, "Scooter! The ball! Run!"

But it never happened. In the outfield, if you are good, you develop an internal clock. You learn the pace of each pitcher, the rhythm of the game itself. Scooter Wells never missed a pitch. And at the crack of the bat, he was on his horse and giddyup gone.

Scooter saw that Clemente got under the ball. He missed the sweet spot not by an inch, as the baseball expression goes ("It's a game of inches," the announcers always intone), but by a far smaller fraction. A hair, perhaps. But you'll never hear a commentator on ESPN say, "It's a game of hairs."

It would sound too gross.

Now the ill-treated ball, so rudely bashed, travels in a soaring arc toward the right-center field gap. Scooter Wells, part physicist, part Labrador retriever, bolts toward the fence. "It's mine! It's mine!" he pointlessly yells, for the ball can be no one else's. At full gallop, Scooter's hat flies off his head. He extends his arm and snares Clemente's bomb in the webbing of his glove.

Inning over.

No runs, no errors, one hit, two stolen bases, one wonderful catch, and half a dozen heart attacks in the stands. Five more innings to go.

3

Top of the Second

	1	2	3	4	5	6	R	H	E
VISITORS	0	-					0	0	0
HOME	0						0	1	0

Way to go get it, Scooter!" an elated Coach Van Zant greets the team as they filter into the dugout. Reading the scorebook from over the shoulder of Alex's dad, Mr. Lionni, who often serves as the team's scorekeeper and statistician, Coach Van Zant calls out, "We've got Harris, The Right Sweeney, and Scooter Wells coming up. Max Young—you're in the hole." And then Coach Van Zant says what he always says after calling out the lineup, "Sounds like a run to me!"

Carter Harris pulls on a helmet, grabs a bat, and waits at the on-deck circle, like a fast car idling at a red light. Carter is a great shortstop, a good pitcher, and the best all-around ballplayer on Earl Grubb's Pool Supplies. He wears his hair thick, long, blond, and wild, as if he's never seen a comb. He glances at his mother in the stands. There's something about the expression on her face. The way she bites her nails. For one instant, Carter wonders if something is wrong. Or, well, no. For an instant, just a flash, he doesn't wonder. Carter *knows*. Something is wrong.

This familiar sense of unease, of trouble right around the corner, has afflicted Carter for as long as he can remember. Not that his friends would ever know it. Carter is careful to keep that part of him hidden, his secret heart.

No matter how hard he tries, Carter Harris cannot remember the day his father died. He knows the details, he's heard the stories countless times. Carter was not yet eighteen months old when police officer Patrick Harris left for work to never return again. He was shot during what was a routine traffic stop in downtown Albany, and died right there on the street, three bullets in his chest. Just like that: gone.

Carter could not remember, though he dared not admit it, the last time he saw his father. Did he kiss him good-bye? Give him a hug? Did he even notice when the screen door clicked shut, and his uniformed father walked out of his life forever? Carter had no answers to those questions. Just an emptiness, an absence. Yet he returned to those questions again and again, the way a tongue feels for the spot of a missing tooth, probing the sore gums, pushing, reaching for what is not there.

**Leading off the top of the second inning,
it's shortstop Carter Harris. . . .**

It was a bad at-bat. No other way to describe it. A give-away, as some players called it. You swing at the bad pitches, take the good ones, and you are out before your mind clears. That's how Carter felt, skulking back to the bench, helmet tumbling to the ground. Out on three pitches, the third one a meatball down the heart of the plate. For some reason, Carter froze up, didn't swing. Strike three. Grab some pine, son.

That's baseball. It happens.

Still, a dark cloud drifted over Carter like a bad mood, and with it the threat of rain. Alone on the bench, Carter thinks, *Something's off*. But he can't put his finger on it.

That's four batters, four strikeouts for Nick Clemente, who has started off this game on fire. Next up, it's, um, which Sweeney is that? Ah, Eamon Sweeney, playing left field and batting fifth. Only their mother can tell them apart. . . .

As Eamon crosses toward the plate, Mike sees his late-arriving parents squeezing themselves into the stands. His sister isn't with them. She won't come. Not to *his* game. And later on, home from starring on her own team, Candace will have a perfectly good reason. How she wanted to, but couldn't. *Blah, blah, blah*. Mike tells himself that he doesn't care, a cloak of indifference he wears like a protective shell. He holds it snug to his heart: *I don't care*. As if by saying so, Mike could make it true, and in making it true, could somehow come to believe it.

Coach Reid puts on the bunt, anything to shake things up, to snap this string of deflating strikeouts. Eamon receives the sign, feels a wave of disappointment, tugs at his jersey, steps into the batter's box, taps home plate with the end of his bat.

The fastball is on him quickly. Eamon bunts the pitch too hard, too straight. Clemente hops off the mound, picks up the ball, and throws to first. Eamon, running hard, is out by twenty feet.

Sam Reiser marks the play in his scorebook, "1–3," pitcher to first base. Sam's father calls scorekeeping "the lost art," and bemoans how "kids today" don't know how to keep score properly. He made sure it wasn't true in the Reiser household. Sam has never seen a major league game without a scorebook on his lap and a stubby pencil in his hand.

Though Eamon's bunt wasn't successful, Sam liked the *idea* of it. At least they forced Northeast to make a play. By this time, it has become obvious to Sam that he is pulling hard for the boys on Earl Grubb's Pool Supplies. Sam hopes that his voice won't betray his feelings. Maybe professional announcers could be impartial, but not Sam. Still, he wants to be fair; it's his job. So he leans into the microphone and keeps it simple:

Center fielder Billy—Scooter—Wells. . . .

"Hey, Scooter." It's Max Young's urgent voice. "Save my ups, huh?"

That's the thought of every good hitter who's on-deck with two outs. *Save my ups. Keep the inning alive. Come on, give me a chance, I can hit this guy.*

Scooter takes the first three pitches and gets ahead in the count, 2–1. He takes the fourth pitch, just a touch outside, for ball three. Catcher Travis Green holds the ball in his glove for an exaggerated moment. *It was right there,* he pantomimes to the umpire in silent protest. Then he snaps the ball back to his pitcher.

Clemente huffs in disapproval. "You're squeezing me, blue," he complains to the home-plate umpire.

Scooter steps out of the box. The count has worked in his favor. He thinks, *Three and one, hitter's count. Look fastball.* Scooter is right about the next pitch and rips it down the right-field line, foul by about ten inches.

"Straighten it out, Scooter," Coach Reid beckons.

Scooter gets the barrel of the bat on the full-count pitch, but is a touch behind the fastball. He grounds it sharply to first base, where the ball is scooped up by first baseman Steven Smith, who takes it to the bag unassisted.

In the dugout, Max Young sighs, takes off his helmet, slides his bat into the rack unused, grabs his glove, and heads out to second base.

4

Bottom of the Second

	1	2	3	4	5	6	R	H	E
VISITORS	0	0					0	0	0
HOME	0	-					0	1	0

On the bench during warm-ups, the three scrubeenies—Sweeney, Wong, and Weinberg—chat amiably about video games, paintball battles, funny nicknames, dirt bikes, and Jessica Simpson. Colin Sweeney eyes the field. He counts the players, then looks into the opposing dugout. "Where's Mednick? I don't see Mednick," he says. Sweeney shouts to the opposing team's first-base coach, "Hey, Carbinowski! Where's Mednick?"

Marty Carbinowski, standing in the first-base coach's box, digs a finger in his ear. He shrugs with indifference. *Dunno.*

"What are you digging for, Carbinowski? You got gold in them thar ears?" Sweeney shouts.

Wong and Weinberg chuckle. They love it when Colin

gets on a roll. Even if he never gets a hit, Colin is good for the team. He keeps things light.

Carbinowski continues to root around in his right ear, his thick index finger screwed halfway into his skull. He eventually removes it, furtively glancing at the tip of his finger, his eyes on the prize.

"Watch Carbinowski," Colin whispers to his gleeful cohorts, Wong and Weinberg. "He's going to eat it. I know it. Carbinowski is an earwax-eating weirdo, I'm telling ya."

The three boys—like owls on a limb—watch Marty Carbinowski as he holds a curled index finger near his face for inspection, turning it this way and that.

"Eat it," Colin murmurs softly. "Eat it, eat it. Come on, Carbinowski, you big ape—suck on that finger!"

All said scarcely above a whisper, heard only by Wong and Weinberg, who won't be subbed into the game until the end of two innings, according to local Little League rules.

Carbinowski eyeballs the waxy deposit on the tip of his finger, so close to the tip of his tongue, like a word he can't quite recall. He casually scans the field, the stands, the opposing dugout, where he spies three sets of owlish eyes staring directly at him, hooting in anticipation. Carbinowski blanches and wipes his finger on his baseball pants.

"Ewwwwww!" Colin roars, hysterical.

A moment later, he jumps up and is at Coach Reid's shoulder. "Mednick's not here," Colin says.

Coach Reid blinks, checks the scorebook with Mr. Lionni. "Nope, must be out sick or something," he replies.

Colin is disappointed in Coach Reid's reaction. Everybody knows that Jasper Mednick is the worst player in the league, very possibly the worst player in the history of organized baseball. He can't hit, he can't catch, and he runs as if he's dragging a sack of bricks. Mednick wasn't slow, he was glacial. Global-warming slow. Ice caps melted faster. Mednick was good for two errors and a couple of strikeouts a game, guaranteed. It was a blow that Mednick couldn't attend the championship game. Not to mention suspicious.

"Maybe Clemente told him the wrong field," Colin opines.

"Sit down, Colin," Coach Van Zant says, his voice betraying a hint of annoyance. "Don't worry about who's here and who's not here. Watch the game."

Reid and Van Zant lock eyes. "Still, I wouldn't put it past Clemente, you know," Jeff Reid tells his fellow coach.

A soft snicker alerts the men to the fact that Colin Sweeney hasn't moved a muscle. "Maybe I should check to see if Mednick is trapped in the bathroom," he suggests. "I'd feel a whole lot better if I saw Mednick out there in right field, picking dandelions."

"The bench, Colin," Coach Van Zant says, smiling. "Sit on it."

Sweeney returns to his seat, sliding between Wong and Weinberg. "Mednick ain't coming," he mutters. "It isn't fair."

"Bummer," Wong concludes.

"I'll say," Weinberg agrees. "Mednick sucks."

"He sucks socks," Sweeney says, smiling. Then pauses,

considering things. "He sucks sweaty socks . . . on Saturdays."

"Today is Saturday," Patrick Wong notes.

"All day," Colin replies. "Wow, no Mednick. Now we might actually have to get hits and everything if we want to win this game."

"If?" Patrick queries.

"I'm just saying," Colin grumbles. "We'd be a lot better off if Mednick was here, screwing things up for the bad guys."

Here's Steven Smith, looking to get things started in the bottom half of the second inning. . . .

Way out in front of a curveball, Smith grounds softly to Sanchez at third for the first out. That's always big, something that Dylan's father drummed into his head for years: "You've got to get that leadoff hitter," he advised his son. Well, mission accomplished.

Batting sixth, Owen Finkel. . . .

Finkel is another big kid—the Northeast team seems to have a lot of them—and he bats from the left side.

"Lefty!" Branden calls out. He stands and holds up his right hand, gesturing toward the right-field line. Scooter Wells in center and Mike Tyree in right slide over about ten steps, while Max Young shifts toward the hole between first and second. Alex Lionni at first plays deep and close to the line. Big left-handed sluggers like Finkel will always get a first baseman's attention. Satisfied with the defensive alignment, Branden gets set behind the plate.

On the third pitch, Finkel lofts a lazy fly toward the line in right field. Mike Tyree drifts over, pounds his glove, settles under it. A can of corn. Two away.

Sam Reiser smiles to himself. *Real smooth*, he thinks, admiring Mike's easy grace. Sam checks the lineup and says into the microphone:

Now up, catcher Travis Green. . . .

Despite the two quick outs, Dylan isn't happy. He doesn't like his fastball today, it won't go where he wants it. He sees Travis come to the plate and the two boys can't help but sneak a grin at each other. They are friends, they take a few classes together in middle school, and sit with the same sprawling group in the cafeteria. Perhaps because it was the last image in his mind—lunch at school—Dylan serves up a meatball. Travis puts a textbook swing on it. Front leg locked, back leg bent, hips open, head down: The ball stops rolling at the fence, where Scooter picks it up and fires to Nando at third base, holding Green to a stand-up double.

Now the Northeast dugout comes alive, thrilled to have a base runner in scoring position. "Yeah, yeah, yeah!" Ausanio cries, clapping his hands together. "Travis, you rock!"

Dylan can't help himself: He glances at his dad, shrugs helplessly. Dylan steps off the mound and rubs the ball in his hands. He checks the batter due up next. It's Joey Crocker.

Not a great hitter, but Crocker can flat-out fly. Dylan has seen Crocker beat out routine grounders to the infield, pounding the ball into the grass and then simply outrunning the play. He checks Carter at short, who has already moved in a couple of steps.

"Not a problem," Carter assures Dylan. "Two outs, Dill. You go get him. We're good."

Now batting, Joey Crocker. . . .

Crocker is all high-twitch energy at the plate, a sinewy string bean with slender calves and a long torso. Dylan decides to pound him inside with fastballs and quickly gets two strikes. Crocker chokes up, crouches lower. He's willing to shorten his swing to put the ball in play—anything not to whiff.

Dylan has him set up for the curveball low and away, but bounces it in the dirt. Branden can't handle it. The ball rolls to the backstop. Green cruises into third without a throw. The go-ahead run is now sixty feet from home.

The next pitch is low. The count runs to 2–2. Travis Green dances down the line between third and home, itching to score; Branden bluffs a throw to Nando at third, then gets the ball back to his pitcher. "Let's go, Dill, right now!" he shouts. "Make your pitch."

Dylan looks to the sky, takes a deep breath, and again casts his eyes around the infield. He sees Carter inch forward, leaning on the balls of his feet. It's a sight that gives a pitcher confidence.

45

"One more strike, Dilly-Dill!"

"Let's go, number twelve."

"Come on, Dylan, let's get out of this."

The southpaw begins his windup. . . .

Now a lot of guys all over the planet play shortstop. Anybody can stand there. They catch the ball, make good throws, get the routine outs. But there are certain plays that separate the true shortstops from the guys who just fill the position. The backhand play in the hole, for example, when he ranges to his right, plucks the hard bouncer from the turf, and plants his right foot to make the long overhand throw to first. Not too many guys make that play. Then there's the little flare into the outfield where the shortstop has to run with his back to the plate, desiring to snatch the ball before it falls back to earth, fearlessly risking collision with a hard-charging outfielder. And then there's the play that happens next, the slow four-hopper past the mound, the play that shortstops call "do or die."

Carter Harris is about to show everyone whether he's something special, or just another guy playing the game's most unforgiving position.

On the field, baseball is a game of isolation, nine singular outposts of shared solitude, for every player is ultimately alone. You are a "team" immediately before and after each play. You wear the same uniform, you lift up and support each other. But in the decisive moment, when games are won and lost, no one else can catch the ball for you. In everyday life, however, sometimes there's a helping hand.

Growing up without a father, Carter inevitably drew close to his uncle Jimmy, older brother to his mother. Uncle Jimmy was a cop, just like Carter's dad. On many weekends, especially during spring and summer, Carter and his mother would drive across town to visit. They'd bring food, or pull out the gas grill, play cards, catch a game on TV, just hang out. It was nice; Carter liked it. Uncle Jimmy was family.

Best of all, Uncle Jimmy always had a little something for Carter. Usually a pack of baseball cards. Topps, always Topps. Uncle Jimmy frowned at the other brands. During every visit, Uncle Jimmy would give Carter a conspiratorial tap, jerk his head, and say something like, "You gotta come see what I got the other day, Carter."

Carter would follow Jimmy into a small back room, which in most suburban houses would be a den with a big-screen television, but in Uncle Jimmy's place it contained what he called "the gallery," his baseball memorabilia collection. Uncle Jimmy was a genuine fanatic when it came to his collection. It was his hobby and his passion.

The room featured treasures of every description. Carter would gaze in dumbstruck wonder as Uncle Jimmy, tall and thick around the middle, hair a shock of faded yellow, would proudly show off his latest acquisition: an authentic glove used by Dominic DiMaggio, a baseball signed by Bob Feller, a jersey worn by some obscure Cardinal infielder.

Uncle Jimmy collected cards, too. His prized card was a 1957 Topps Ted Williams in mint condition. "Spent a lot of money on this bad boy," Uncle Jimmy would say, winking at Carter. "Too much." Jimmy explained to Carter every aspect of card collecting, including how to properly judge the condition of cards. "Ideally, you want sharp corners," Uncle Jimmy told Carter, "nothing fuzzy or soft. The color should be bright and clear, the borders well-centered. And you don't want scratches, stains, or creases. Unless," he said, pausing, "none of that stuff matters to you. Sometimes I love a beat-up old card. A card that you can tell has been loved, know what I'm saying, Carter? Touched and flipped and handled—stared at, read over and over—not stuffed away in some musty box, never to be touched. That old card may not be worth a lot on eBay, but if you love it, Carter, maybe that's worth a lot more than money. You know what I'm saying?"

After Carter had eyeballed Jimmy's latest treasure, his uncle often handed him a fresh pack of baseball cards. "Go on, open it," he'd urge, still eager after all these years, still a boy at heart. "Who'd ya get?"

Unmarried, without children of his own, Uncle Jimmy figured he had love to spare, so he poured it over his nephew like a cooler of Gatorade, just splashed it down on Carter's head. Jimmy Gallagher knew he could never fill the shoes left behind by Carter's father. But still, he'd try them on every once in a while, walk around in them, be that father to the boy who had none. And most times, Carter let him, glad for it.

They were a team.

Up in the announcer's booth, Sam Reiser watches the play unfold, his mind struggling to absorb the sudden rush of activity. Crocker swings and tops the ball into the ground, trickling a slow roller to the right side of the mound. The base runner at third, Green, instantly breaks for home. Crocker flings his bat and bolts out of the box like a shot. Dylan Van Zant dives for the ball but it's out of reach.

Carter Harris charges. He's on the grass, moving fast. Carter knows there's no time to hesitate. Out of the corner of his eye, he sees Green heading for home—there's no play there. And now Carter is in the tunnel, charging a baseball, and that's all the world he sees, that bouncing white globe. He is deaf to the shouts, the cries from the stands. He can't wait for a good hop. It's now or never, do or die. Without thinking, Carter bends low and short-hops the ball with his bare hand, takes one step, another, and throws across his body as he pushes off on his right foot, tumbling to the ground as he releases the ball.

Crocker races toward the bag, going all-out. First baseman Alex Lionni stretches for the ball. Crocker leans forward . . . his foot hits the bag as the ball reaches the glove . . . and the umpire raises his right fist, thumb extended.

"Out!" he cries.

5

Top of the Third

	1	2	3	4	5	6	R	H	E
VISITORS	O	O	-				O	O	O
HOME	O	O					O	2	O

Everyone pounds Carter on the back—"Who is that guy?!" roars Colin Sweeney, racing out of the dugout to congratulate his teammate—and even Mr. Lionni taps the scorebook with a pencil in excitement.

According to the rules, every player has to play the field for a minimum of four innings. It's time to make substitutions. After a quick conference with Coach Reid, Mr. Lionni gives the changes to Sam Reiser in the announcer's booth, calling up to the open, second-story window:

"Colin Sweeney in for Wells in the sixth spot . . . Weinberg in for Young in the seventh spot . . . and Wong in for Tyree below that."

"Got it," Sam answers, carefully noting the changes in his scorecard.

Coach Clemente, down a player due to Mednick's absence, makes only two changes: Dross in for Smith, Carbinowski in for Crocker.

The revised lineups now read:

• VISITORS •
Earl Grubb's Pool Supplies

PLAYERS	Pos.
Dylan Van Zant	P
Nando Sanchez	3B
Branden Reid	C
Carter Harris	SS
Eamon Sweeney	LF
Colin Sweeney	CF
Tyler Weinberg	RF
Patrick Wong	2B
Alex Lionni	1B

Northeast Gas & Electric

PLAYERS	Pos.
Justin Pinkney	SS
Frank Ausanio	CF
Angel Tatis	3B
Nick Clemente	P
Luther Dross	RF
Owen Finkel	LF
Travis Green	C
Marty Carbinowski	1B
Billy Thompson	2B

"I'm sorry you didn't get a chance to hit," Coach Reid apologizes to Max Young. "It's tough when no one gets on base."

A flicker of a frown crosses Max's face. He says he understands, while at the same time showing that he isn't thrilled, either.

"You'll be back in the game the fifth inning," Coach Reid assures the young player. "We're going to need you, Max. Believe me, you're going to get a big at-bat before this game is through."

Max nods.

"How's the pitching arm feel today?"

"Fine," Max answers.

"I might need you in relief today," Coach Reid tells him. "Stay loose."

Max glances into the dugout at Dylan. "I'll be ready," he says.

"Can you coach first base?"

"Yeah, sure," Max replies. Five seconds later, he stands in the coach's box, clapping his hands for the leadoff hitter.

We're set to start the third inning. No score so far, just goose eggs. Leading off for Earl Grubb's Pool Supplies, it's Red Bull, Tyler Weinberg. . . .

Baseball is many things to many people, but for Tyler Weinberg the game can be reduced to one elementary act: swinging the bat. Tyler loves to hit. He is a graduate of the "grip it and rip it" school of hitting; he swings for the fences every time. And he doesn't care who's pitching. Because once the hurler throws his pitch, at the moment when the ball slips from his fingertips, baseball becomes the simplest game in the world: Tyler against the ball, floating in space. His objective? Kill it. Smash that sucker to smithereens.

Watching Tyler eagerly step to the plate, Sam grins inwardly, remembering a story that Mrs. Weinberg told at Tyler's last birthday party. Tyler was just a toddler, she had explained, still in diapers. One day he was outside playing with a stick. Even then, his mother said, Tyler liked smashing things. Well, he was out there for a while—*whap, whap, whap*—rapping that big stick against anything and everything.

Suddenly Mrs. Weinberg heard a dull thud, *oomphff*, followed by Tyler's joyous laughter. She rushed outside to discover Tyler, grinning triumphantly, holding a dead squirrel by the tail.

"Ty-Ty smash," he explained proudly.

And now he stood at home plate, glaring at pitcher Nick Clemente, an aluminum bat in his meaty grip, eager to swing and swing again. To batter, bash, smash, and shatter. The boy who liked to clobber things. Broken lamps, cracked windows, whatever was in his path. Especially, and most happily, baseballs.

Tyler swings and misses at a fastball ten inches above his head. This mistake elicits a chorus of advice from the stands:

"Make him throw strikes, Ty!"

"Don't help him out!"

"Lay off the high ones, Ty!"

Such is the life of a Little Leaguer. There's no shortage of helpful suggestions.

In the batter's box, Tyler is deaf to them all. He swings and misses for strike two. It pains him, for he longs to pulverize the red-stitched orb. Tyler grips the bat tighter, clenches his teeth, angry at the ball itself, that stinking white rock! He stands at the plate, oblivious to everything except that baseball, bad intentions in his heart. He eyes Clemente, thinking, *Come on, come on. Bring it!*

On the next pitch, Tyler sends a frozen rope into left field. But the ball flies directly to Owen Finkel. The outfielder doesn't move a step. Finkel catches the liner without incident. Big applause from fans and teammates, a tremor of relief ripples across Nick Clemente's face.

Tyler, for his part, finds this turn of events outrageous and unfair. He storms into the dugout, railing over the injustice. "I was robbed," he protests.

Wow, that was a rocket. Nice grab by Finkel. Seven up and seven down for Nick Clemente. Now up, Patrick Wong. . . .

In his approach as a hitter, Patrick Wong is Tyler's mirror image. While Tyler will swing at anything he can reach (and some things he can't), Patrick goes to the plate in hopes of working out a walk. He's learned that bad things happen when he swings the bat. Or, more accurately, no "thing" happens at all—except an ever-so-slight breeze caused by a bat slicing pointlessly (and aimlessly) through the air. So he keeps the useless aluminum on his shoulder, watching pitch after pitch. He is, as they say, a looker. And Nick Clemente knows it.

Patrick takes a ball. He takes a strike. He takes another strike.

"Come on, Patrick, you've got to swing that bat!" calls an exasperated Coach Reid, who has watched this scenario play out game after game. It is, for Jeff Reid, his great failure as a coach this season. He hoped to turn Patrick Wong into a decent hitter. At the very least, get the boy to swing the bat. And to this end, he has failed spectacularly. "Just like at practice, Patrick," he calls from the third-base coach's box. His voice encouraging, almost pleading. "You can do it!"

No, Patrick thinks, *I can't.*

So he goes down looking, strike three.

Patrick thinks, *Lousy umpire.*

Batting ninth, Alex Lionni. . . .

Alex requests time and adjusts his square-shaped, shatter-proof goggles.

Two years ago, Alex had been in the worst slump of his life. He was either striking out or beating grounders into the dirt. Teammates had even started to call him "The Wormkiller."

After the games, he wouldn't talk. He couldn't talk. Alex sat in silence during the car ride home, grunting answers to his mother's questions, staring out the window as the vinyl-sided houses slid past. He usually showered and went to his room, frustrated and confused.

Why couldn't he hit? What had happened to him?

When Alex's father offered to give Alex some extra batting practice, Alex stifled a laugh. His father was the world's biggest spaz. The thought of his father, Casper Lionni, trying to pitch was comical. The guy lived in a suit and tie, his sharp, thin nose stuck in a book. He hated sports.

On the following evening, the two of them drove to the park. Predictably, the first few pitches were pathetic. The balls bounced in the dirt, went over Alex's head, or fluttered behind him like blind moths. Then, after moving (danger-ously) closer, Mr. Lionni sailed a fat one right in there.

Alex swung wildly and missed. Probably, Alex reasoned, from the shock of seeing his father throw a strike. His dad threw a baseball the way another man might throw a dart. Just a little stab-step and a flick of the wrist. No windup at all. Alex thought he looked bizarre, ridiculous. But he was getting the ball over the plate. And it was good to swing the bat.

They paused to round up the baseballs. Alex had missed a lot of pitches, while beating others into the dirt.

"Maybe it's my back elbow," Alex hypothesized.

"Try to swing under the ball," his father suggested. "When you miss, you always seem to be swinging on top of it."

That was, of course, the most ridiculous batting instruction Alex had ever heard. He knew to open his hips, keep his hands high, squash the bug, head on the ball, and all the other tips about hitting one could garner from books, private lessons, baseball camps, videos, and more.

But somehow his father's advice worked. Once Alex concentrated on hitting the bottom part of the ball, he began to spray line drives all over the field. It was amazing. Alex was stunned, hitting was fun again.

A half hour later, while piling the gear into the trunk, Alex thanked his father. "I think you cured me," he said.

"Actually, no," his father answered. "But I think I know the cause of your problem."

"Yeah?"

Mr. Lionni removed the glasses from his face. "Try these," he said.

Alex put on the squarish, thick-framed glasses. To his surprise, the world appeared a little sharper, clearer. He looked at his father in amazement.

"It's my fault, I suppose. Bad genetics," Mr. Lionni told Alex. "I'm afraid you need glasses."

Come on, Alex," Mr. Lionni calls, pushing with his middle finger against a pair of dark-rimmed glasses.

Alex is down 1–2 in the count, but he feels relaxed, like he's close to timing Clemente's heater. Alex serves the next pitch to the opposite field, a sharp line drive to right, snapping Clemente's string of eight consecutive outs.

Outfielder Luther Dross moves unsteadily to the ball and it skips under his glove, rolling to the right-field corner.

"Go, go!" yells Max Young from the coach's box. "Think three, think three!"

Alex cuts the bag at second and doesn't slow down. He picks up Coach Reid at third base, waving him on. Dross recovers the ball and hurls it wildly in the direction of Northeast second baseman Billy Thompson. There's no throw to third. Alex Lionni pulls in safely with a triple. Or, according to official scorer Sam Reiser, a single and a two-base error.

The boys in the Earl Grubb's dugout leap to their feet, cheering enthusiastically.

Up in the booth, Sam wants to jump to his feet, too. He feels exhilarated—*What a huge error by Dross!*—and fights back a desire to pace back and forth, climb the walls, soar. Instead he sits in his chair, does his job, and announces the next batter.

That's the first base runner of the game for Earl Grubb's Pool Supplies. Nick Clemente will now be working to preserve the shutout. Due up, pitcher Dylan Van Zant. . . .

Sam turns his full attention to the study of Nick Clemente. He wants to see how the burly pitcher reacts to the error. The best pitchers have a way of shrugging off a teammate's mistake. They don't get upset, they don't point fingers. Usually, they do the opposite; they accept that errors (like umpires) are a part of the game's complex tapestry, its warp and woof, and they go after the next hitter with everything they've got.

But there will always be pitchers who react poorly, so Sam watches Clemente with fixed fascination, because he *always* watches the pitcher immediately after an error. Clemente steps off the mound, paws the dirt with his cleats, slams the ball into his glove, growls, mutters to himself. He's like a mean dog on a short leash. To Sam's keen eye, the Northeast twirler looks rattled.

So it comes as no surprise to Sam when Nick Clemente's next pitch is a hanging curveball. The pitch looks to batter Dylan Van Zant like a beach ball imprinted with the words KICK ME in fluorescent letters. Dylan's eyes widen . . . and he calmly shoots the ball into center field for an RBI single.

Alex Lionni crosses the plate, greeted by a jubilant Nando Sanchez and, in turn, mobbed by the entire team. Earl Grubb's Pool Supplies take the lead, one run to nothing.

Even better, Sam Reiser notes to himself, they have punctured a hole in Nick Clemente's balloon. *Hiss.* It's the sound of air escaping.

Deflated, Clemente fumes, kicks the dirt. *It's not my fault,* he simmers. *That run never scores if Luther catches the freaking ball.* Clemente glowers disdainfully at right field, shooting daggers at Luther Dross. The remorseful right fielder is an eleven-year-old boy, young for this team, a fifth-grader who has committed the crime of imperfection.

That is, Luther Dross is just like everybody else. Try as he might, Luther screws up every once in a while. And all he wants to do, out there in right field, is hide under a rock. Even so, a small part of Luther thinks, *Screw you, Clemente. I made an error. Get over it.*

Earl Grubb's takes the lead, one to nothing. Now batting, Nando Sanchez. . . .

Clemente unleashes his frustration on the next hitter, Nando Sanchez. Clemente grunts loudly, a wounded-animal sound, pouring his aggression into each pitch. He wants to throw even harder. But because he's a pitcher, and not a linebacker, his anger has the opposite effect. In an effort to get more, he achieves less. Coaches call it "muscling up." Instead of throwing in a loose, liquid motion, the muscles constrict, the body tightens, and the fastball loses velocity. You can't play baseball with steam pouring out of your ears.

Nando battles to a 2–2 count, fouling off four pitches along the way.

"Yeah, Nando! *Bueno, bueno!*" voices in the stands cry in approval. That's his family, Nando knows, with him on every pitch.

"Straighten it out, Nando."

"He can't get you out, Nando!"

"You are right on it!"

Another foul ball, straight back. Clemente shakes his head. He should be able to bury this guy. The Earl Grubb's team, every last player, stands on the edge of the dugout, fully engaged.

"Let's go, kiiiiiiiid," Mike Tyree calls.

Nando foul tips the next pitch back into Travis Green's glove. Travis squeezes the ball for strike three, the final out of the inning.

Disheartened, Nando looks from the catcher's glove to his father in the stands. "Hey, hey, chin up," Mr. Sanchez calls. He claps his hands twice and smiles proudly. "Great at-bat, Nando! Way to battle."

And he's right. Even Nando's strikeout feels like a small victory. He fought off every pitch, stood toe-to-toe with Clemente, and didn't yield an inch. Another pinprick in the balloon.

· 6 ·

Bottom of the Third

	1	2	3	4	5	6	R	H	E
VISITORS	0	0	1				1	2	0
HOME	0	0	-				0	2	1

Coach Reid, is it okay if I go to the bathroom?" asks Mike Tyree.

"You're not in the game, right?"

"Nope."

Coach Jeff Reid looks toward the concession building, then up to the announcer's booth on the second floor. "Maybe if you get a minute," he says, "you could check on him if you'd like."

Mike smiles, knows exactly who Coach Reid is talking about. "Well, yeah, sure. I was kind of thinking about it. Do you mind?"

"Just don't take all day," Coach Reid says. "We've got a pretty good game going so far."

Mike grins. "Yeah, I noticed." Mike glances into the dugout. Max Young is seated in the far corner of the bench, watching as Dylan completes his warm-ups. Scooter Wells rummages in his bat bag, quietly rapping the lyrics to a Jay-Z tune. Mike opens the gate, steps through, clicks it shut, and leaves the field behind.

There's a squarish, two-story building—an overachieving shed, really—that is directly behind home plate, separated by the backstop. It houses the concession stand on the ground floor. Decent hot dogs and french fries, but stay away from the nachos unless you like the idea of plastic cheese poured in clumps over cardboard chips. Plus you have to watch who's at the grill before ordering. Some of those people can turn a cheeseburger into something unrecognizable. Or as Colin Sweeney once famously observed, "Not of this earth." And when Mr. Gabruzzi is at the grill, he sweats like a bricklayer in July. *Drip, drip, sizzle, sizzle.* Kills your appetite in a heartbeat.

There's a side door that opens to a crowded supply room, cluttered with gear of all kinds. A "Lost and Found" that amounts to a big cardboard box of assorted crap that nobody bothers to claim. Go up the stairs and there's a narrow room with a large window overlooking the field. The press box, if you want to call it that. There's a countertop at the window, before an untidy row of gray metal folding chairs. On the counter there's an old box of pencils, some half-empty soda cans, napkins nobody ever thinks to use, Sam's cell phone, and a microphone. That's where Sam sits. The cat's seat. The bird's-eye view. Or whatever.

Sam announces one or two games every week, and he takes the job seriously. At first, the rules were very strict: "No editorializing." That meant, just the facts. Who's up, the score, the count, the inning, that kind of thing. Sam didn't mind, exactly, but he had more on his mind. Gradually Sam added a few comments here and there, like, oh, "Sanchez doubled last time up on a 3–2 fastball," or, "Weinberg leads the league with five dingers."

No one seemed to mind, or maybe they didn't notice. Or, more likely, nobody was willing to give Sam Reiser a hard time. How could they? The kid had a free pass. So Sam kept pushing it further, until he pretty much said whatever he wanted.

After games, people would comment, "Good job, Sam." The kids in school noticed, too. Announcing the games gave Sam a little slice of celebrity. He couldn't play on the field—not now, anyway—but as the announcer, he was a part of the game. He had a role. He was still, in a way, a player. He was the voice over the loudspeaker, the storyteller, the soul of the game.

And it is here where Mike Tyree is headed, to see his best friend in the world, been that way since forever, his buddy Sam Reiser.

Billy Thompson steps to the plate. . . .

Inexplicably, Dylan can't throw a strike. He falls behind light-hitting Thompson 3–0. Steps off the mound, takes off his cap, wipes his forehead with a sleeve, untucks and tucks his jersey, spits, frowns, looks to his father.

"Don't give in, Dill. Make your pitch," Coach Van Zant says from the dugout. "This is the guy you've got to get. Give me that first out."

Dylan throws a strike. Thompson gets good metal on the following 3–1 pitch, raps a hard grounder to third. Nando Sanchez glides to his left, cradles the ball, throws a strike to Alex at first base.

One away in the bottom of the third inning. Now it's back around to the top of the order, Justin Pinkney. . . .

From his chair in the announcer's booth, Sam watches as Dylan throws two balls to Pinkney. Neither come near the plate.

Mike steps into the room, plops down in a chair beside Sam. "Nice view, huh?"

"It's better down there," Sam replies.

Mike considers this, lets the remark pass without offering. He can't disagree.

"You need anything?" Mike asks. "Some curly fries, something to drink?"

"No, I'm fine. I've got some peanut M&M's," Sam says, pointing to the yellow bag on the counter.

Mike helps himself to a handful.

"That was a nice catch before," Sam notes.

Mike nods.

"I see your folks made it," Sam says.

"Yeah, I just talked to them," Mike says. His voice flat. Giving nothing away.

"That's good, right?"

"Yeah, I guess. My dad wanted to know why I wasn't in the game."

Ball three, in the dirt.

The two friends sit lost in their separate thoughts. They watch through the pane as the game unfolds below.

"Are you doing anything after the game?" Mike asks.

"Yeah," Sam quips, "I'm planning on setting a new world's record on my pogo stick."

Mike smirks, pauses. "My sister has a basketball game after this, and I really don't feel like going. Thing is, my parents aren't going to let me stay home alone." He looks at Sam, measuring his reaction the way a carpenter might study a door frame. Mike complains, "I hate getting dragged to her games all the time."

Sam knows what Mike is trying to ask. "Look, Mike, I'm not feeling like much fun these days."

"We could just hang out," Mike offers, "play a video game or something. Sit and talk, take it easy, whatever."

Sam shakes his head. "Not today. I'm fried."

"Sure," Mike answers softly. "I understand."

Dylan Van Zant issues a four-pitch walk to Pinkney.

Sam watches Pinkney jog to first base. Sam feels

distracted, his attention diverted. He just wants to be left alone to watch the game. Is that too much to ask? Mike's presence oppresses him, jangles his nerves. Sam yawns, suddenly tired.

Here's Frank Ausanio, looking for his second hit of the day. . . .

Ausanio goes after the first pitch—a fastball at shoulder level—and skies it into the clouds.

"I got it, I got it!" yells Alex Lionni. He settles under the pop fly a few feet behind the first-base bag. Alex underhands the ball to Dylan, wheels around, and raises two fingers. "Two away!"

"That's a relief," Mike comments to Sam. "Ausanio's a beast."

Sam holds up a finger for silence, leans into the microphone, pushes a black button. . . .

Two outs, Angel Tatis is the batter. . . .

Mike stands, and tilts his head toward the door. "So, um."

"You've got a game to play," Sam says, eyes on the field, his back to Mike. "Better get with your team."

"Yeah, I should. . . ." Mike scans the drab room, the half-filled water bottle, the bag of M&M's on the counter. "Do you need anything else?" he says to the carpet.

"No, I'm good."

"Are you sure?" Mike offers. "Do you need to, you know, go to the bathroom or something?"

"I don't need your help," Sam snaps, turning to stare at Mike. "I'm so sick of being treated like . . ." His voice drifts off, the sentence unfinished, the flash of anger already fading. Sam takes a breath, sighs. "I'm all set. Really, Mike. Go," he says. "Play."

"Sure, sure." Mike turns to leave.

"Hey," Sam calls after him.

"Yeah?"

"Clemente can't throw gas like this for six innings. You guys will get to him."

Mike shakes his head. "I don't know. He's tough."

"You'll see," Sam assures his friend. "He starts out all pumped up, but he can't keep it up for six innings. The first thing you'll notice is he'll be high with his fastball. Then he'll bounce a curveball in the dirt. Then he'll start cursing to himself. And that's when . . ."

There was a pregnant pause. "That's when . . . *what?!*" Mike asks in exasperation.

Sam smiles. "That's when you've got him."

After a quick strike, Angel Tatis checks his swing on a curveball in the dirt. Justin Pinkney breaks for second. Branden handles the ball cleanly, jumps to his feet, and uncorks a throw to second base. The throw is off-line and six feet short of the bag. Patrick Wong waves at the ball while it scoots past, but Carter Harris backs up the throw.

"Time, blue," Branden calls.

He slowly walks to the mound.

"Not again, Branden," Dylan complains. "All you want to do is have meetings."

"Give me a minute," Branden says, his voice distant.

"What are you . . . ?"

"Give me a minute, okay!" Branden demands.

Dylan looks at his teammate. "Branden, you don't look so good. Your face is pale."

"Just . . . shut up a minute, okay? Please?"

Dylan glances to his coaches, unsure of what to do. "Are you all right?"

"Yeah, just a little dizzy," Branden says.

Coach Reid walks toward the base line. "Is there a problem, boys?"

"No," Branden says. "No problem." He waves his father away and returns to his position behind home plate. It's only the third inning, and Branden doesn't know if there's another long throw left in him.

Angel Tatis rips the next pitch to exactly the worst place on the field—if you are a fan of Northeast Gas & Electric. Shortstop Carter Harris vacuums the errant bullet on one hop, then has all the time in the world to throw out Angel at first.

Colin Sweeney races in from center field and roars, "Who zat guy? Who IS that GUY?!"

Carter laughs, seeks his mother in the stands. She's looking away, searching the parking lot. That's when he remembers.

Where's Uncle Jimmy? He promised he'd come.

One day when Uncle Jimmy was wrestling with a pack of sausages over the grill, Carter poked around the house. Just curious, looking around, hoping to find something to do. Carter opened a closet. And he opened a shoe box that was on the floor, deep in the back—and that's where he found it. Uncle Jimmy's gun. It was black, larger than he'd imagined. Carter, nine years old at the time, lifted the gun out of the box. It was heavy in his hand. He didn't intend to shoot it or do anything dumb. He wasn't stupid; Carter knew that guns were dangerous. But still, he just had to . . . touch it.

"Hey! What you got there?" Uncle Jimmy's voice startled him. Jimmy grabbed the weapon from Carter's hands. "What are you doing, Carter? Don't you ever, ever touch this again!"

He was angry, his voice loud.

"I didn't mean . . ." Carter stammered, trembling.

Uncle Jimmy's face relaxed. His eyes softened. He bent down on one knee. "It's not loaded, see," Uncle Jimmy explained, holding the gun in his hand. "When I saw you with it, I got scared. I didn't mean to yell at ya, Carter. But guns are nothing to fool around with, you know what I'm saying?"

"You're not going to get shot, are you, Jimmy?" Carter asked.

"What? Hey." The question felt like a punch to the solar plexus. It took his breath away. Uncle Jimmy—first detective James Gallagher—felt a wave of sadness wash over him. *Poor kid*, he thought. *He'll never get over it.*

"Are you?" Carter repeated, insistent. "Are you?" His eyes were wet, like stones in the rain, shimmering.

The tears came when Carter felt his uncle's arms wrap around him. Together they heaved and sighed, no longer fighting back the sorrow they both had long ago buried.

"No, Carter, don't worry. I'm very careful on the job," Jimmy's voice whispered, his voice close, warm in Carter's ear.

"You won't leave me?" Carter heard himself ask, the words coming of their own volition, echoing up from some deep place. "You won't ever leave?"

"I promise," his uncle said, though he knew such things could not be promised, should never be promised, for one cannot promise to be lucky, to be fortunate, to never be in the wrong place at the wrong time. You can't promise to live.

"I promise, Carter. You are my special boy," he said. Jimmy's hands went to Carter's face, his thumbs wiping away the tears. He stood, turned away, and ran a sleeve across his own face. Jimmy returned the gun to the shoe box and placed it up on a shelf, high and out of reach. He closed the closet door.

"Come on," he said, touching the back of Carter's neck. "I been meaning to show you what I got for the collection the other day. It's awesome."

Top of the Fourth

	1	2	3	4	5	6	R	H	E
VISITORS	0	0	1	-			1	2	0
HOME	0	0	0				0	2	1

Coach Van Zant eyes the lineup card. "Reid, Harris, the Right Sweeney," he calls out. "Colin, you're in the hole. Sounds like a run to me!"

"Be sure to watch for the signs," Coach Reid reminds his players. "We might try to build a run."

Before Branden steps to the plate, his mother comes to the edge of the dugout. She offers him a blue Powerade.

"Not now, Mom, I've got to hit," he protests.

Naomi Reid hands the bottle to her son. "Be sure to drink it," she says. "And Branden, how's it going?" She touches her shoulder.

"I'm okay." He turns his back and heads to the batter's box.

Leading off the top of the fourth inning, catcher Branden Reid. . . .

Branden swings at a fastball at the knees and pounds it into the ground. Shortstop Justin Pinkney plays it cleanly for the out. This one bothers Branden, because his turn at the plate is over almost without him realizing it. He wasn't focused. Instead, he was thinking about his arm, his mom, and the stupid blue Powerade. She should know he prefers Very Berry.

"That's all right, Branden. You'll get him next time," Coach Van Zant says.

Yeah, whatever, thinks Branden. *It's already the fourth inning. I'm running out of "next times."*

One out. Carter Harris, the fielding star of today's game, steps to the plate. . . .

Carter is the team's cleanup hitter, but for the second time today, he comes to the plate with the bases empty. There's no one to "clean up."

Clemente appears to be back to his dominant self. Still working hard, grunting and fuming, pitching his heart out. Carter respects him; Clemente plays hard. Bright as a brick, but damn, can he play.

To Carter's surprise, Clemente starts him off with three consecutive curveballs. The count goes to two balls and a strike.

"Hitter's count, Carter!"

It's his mother's voice. He glances back, sees her in the stands, hands folded on her lap. She's sitting with Mrs. Van Zant, Mr. Reiser, and the Tyrees. His mind wanders.

There's a framed photograph hanging in Uncle Jimmy's gallery that has always left Carter feeling unsettled. Yet he was drawn to it, oddly attached to it, for reasons he could not explain.

It was an unremarkable photograph, really. Black and white, taken moments after the New York Yankees had defeated the San Francisco Giants in the 1962 World Series. It was autographed by the New York Yankees catcher, Elston Howard. To most people, it was a photograph of a celebration. Five Yankees were in the picture, rushing toward each other, thrilled, jubilant. It's a moment in time that would make a Yankee fan smile, perhaps bittersweetly, for the Bronx Bombers would then go into a decline that would see the pinstriped champions fail to win a Series for the next fifteen years. In Yankee time, that's an eternity.

It was the season when Maury Wills stole a record-setting 104 bases, Mickey Mantle won the AL MVP, Sandy Koufax threw his first no-hitter, and when, to Carter's delight, the top reliever was hilariously named Elroy Face.

The Yankees were, well, the damn Yankees, riding high from a long period of ruthless dominance. (Ruth-less? Yes, but they still had Mantle!) Brilliant, talented, triumphant, insufferable. They traveled the land and left behind a wake of heartbreak. Rooting for the Yankees, Carter believed, was like rooting for a dentist with a drill. Like cheering for Goliath against that pesky twerp with the slingshot. Like hanging around with the school bully.

No, Carter rooted for the little guy, and he always did. If a team was bad, he liked them. If they were terrible, he liked them even more. Most folks prefer to ride the winner's bandwagon. Not Carter. Give him a lovable loser any day of the week and twice on Sunday.

Staring at the photograph on Uncle Jimmy's wall, Carter's eyes inevitably fell on the dejected figure in the foreground, a black man in a San Francisco uniform, head down, forlorn. He appeared to be walking down the third-base line, fifteen feet short of home. Frozen in time, he would never touch the plate. Always close, but never arriving.

Uncle Jimmy explained the circumstances of the photo to Carter. "Pretty great, isn't it?" he said. "Elston Howard signed that for me at a card show, long time ago. Nice man, amazing hands. Very strong."

"Who's that?" Carter asked, pointing to the forsaken Giant.

Uncle Jimmy stroked his chin thoughtfully. "That, I believe, is Matty Alou—one of the three Alou brothers, in fact, along with Jesus and Felipe. One game they all played the outfield together for the San Francisco Giants. Pretty neat, don't you think? Three brothers all in a row, playing in the major leagues."

Carter nodded, eyes fixed on the photograph.

Uncle Jimmy continued. "The World Series came down to a seventh game. In the bottom of the ninth, the Giants trailed by a score of one to nothing. Ralph Terry had pitched a masterpiece. Matty Alou led off with a bunt single. The next two batters struck out, then Willie Mays cracked a double to the outfield, but Alou had to hold at third base."

Carter said, "Okay, runners on second and third, two outs, the ninth inning of the seventh game of the World Series. That's unreal."

Uncle Jimmy smiled and picked up the thread. "So up comes big Willie McCovey, a powerful left-handed slugger who could turn baseballs into sawdust. Very intimidating hitter. Anyway, 'Stretch' McCovey did everything a great slugger could do. He ripped the first pitch to right, foul by a couple of feet. A single wins the Series, you know what I'm saying, Carter, because Mays on second base could fly. McCovey takes the next pitch for a ball. Next pitch, McCovey scalds a line drive—totally crushes it, Carter, a rocket—right into the glove of Yankee second baseman Bobby Richardson.

"Game over," Uncle Jimmy said, tapping his finger on the photo. "That's when this photograph was taken, right after McCovey made the last out in the 1962 World Series."

Carter stared at the photo, absorbing every detail. To him, it confirmed everything he had ever suspected.

The world was not fair.

Not even baseball.

At the mouth of the dugout, the Sweeney twins stand side by side. Eamon due up next, Colin to follow.

"If Carter gets on, I'll bunt him over," Eamon tells his brother. "Then you knock him in."

"All righty, then," Colin says, in a pretty fair imitation of Jim Carrey in *Ace Ventura: Pet Detective*. It was an old movie, but in Colin's estimation, a classic.

Eamon watches Clemente with rapt attention. He whispers to Colin, "Watch for his curveball, especially if he gets two strikes on you."

Colin grins, reminded of a line from one of his favorite foul-mouthed movies, *Major League*. He imitates Pedro Cerrano, the thickly accented, superstitious slugger from the movie: "I cannot hit curveball. Straight ball, I hit it very much. Curveball, bats are afraid."

Eamon looks at his brother, frowns in disbelief. "How do you remember this stuff? You're crazy, anybody ever tell you that?"

"It's been mentioned a few times," Colin replies. "But your problem, Eamon, is you think too much. Stop thinking, and just hit the ball."

Clemente jams Carter with a fastball on the hands. The ball flutters weakly to the mound, a butterfly with a busted wing. Clemente pockets it for the second out. Carter Harris has now struck out and popped lamely to the pitcher. Carter can live with that; he understands that failure is part of the game.

He knows he helps the team in the field. But still, Carter doesn't exactly *like* making outs. He vows, *I'll get him next time.*

Eamon Sweeney batting for the second time today. Eamon bunted unsuccessfully his first trip to the plate. . . .

Eamon guesses curveball on the first pitch, and takes a belt-high fastball for a strike. He looks curveball again, and is late on the fastball. Strike two.

He steps out of the box, scans the field.

"Don't think. Just hit," Colin hollers from the dugout.

Eamon shakes his head, digs a hole with his right foot, gets set for the next pitch. *Okay, don't think*, he tells himself. Eamon swings (insanely!) at a fastball way outside for strike three. *Aaarrgghh!*

Colin meets him on the way to the dugout. "Eamon, why'd you swing at that? You've got to use your head."

Aaarrgghh! squared.

Catching gear in hand, Branden stands beside his father. "Dad, we've got to talk."

"What is it, Branden?"

"It's my arm," Branden confesses. The expression on his face says the rest.

"How bad? Where?"

Branden shows his father the spot, tells him how it only hurts when he throws. Coach Reid mulls it over.

"When did this happen? Last inning?"

78

"No, um, a few days ago."

"A few . . . ?"

"I thought it would get better," Branden says quickly. "Mom said that if I rested it . . ."

"Mom said?" Coach Reid takes off his hat, rakes a hand through his thinning hair. "Do you need to sit out the last couple of innings?"

"No," Branden says. "I want to play. It's just that I'm not so sure about catching."

Coach Reid scans the field, checks the dugout, tries to figure out who's available. He hadn't planned for this. The team's backup catcher is Max Young, but Max is out of the game until the next half inning. Coach Reid doesn't want to pull Carter from short. It's a one-run game. He can't risk putting Nando behind the plate.

"Can you give me one more inning?" he asks.

Branden looks into his father's eyes. "Absolutely," he says.

"Just don't try to throw anybody out," Coach Reid says. "If a runner goes, eat the ball."

Branden nods, then bends to put on the gear.

"How could you *not* tell me?" Jeff Reid complains. "I can't believe you, Branden."

"I had to play, Dad," Branden counters, emotion welling up behind his eyes. "It's the championship game."

Coach Reid instantly regrets his harsh tone. Always toughest on his own kid. "I know, Branden, I know. Here, let me help you with that chest protector. . . ."

· 8 ·

Bottom of the Fourth

	1	2	3	4	5	6	R	H	E
VISITORS	0	0	1	0			1	2	0
HOME	0	0	0	-			0	2	1

Dylan walks to the mound, thinking, *Nine outs. Nine more outs. That's all we need.*

Leading off the home fourth, Nick Clemente. . . .

Dylan works Clemente to perfection. Fastballs on the corners for two quick strikes, climbs the ladder with a fastball in the eyes that Clemente doesn't chase, then comes back with a terrific curveball that breaks down at Clemente's ankles. Clemente waves at the ball and somehow golfs a weak flare over third base for a single. A bloop hit the old-timers call a dying quail.

On the bag at first, Clemente claps his hands fiercely. "There you go, Luther!" he roars. "Drive me in!"

Luther Dross, batting for the first time. . . .

Dylan calmly dispatches the overmatched Dross with three quick strikes. Dylan's fastball is showing extra zip this inning, he's throwing loose and free. The boy on the hill silently counts: *Eight more outs.*

Owen Finkel—he flied to right his first time up. . . .

Out in right field, Tyler Weinberg chews gum (first prize in Colin Sweeney's movie trivia contest) and thinks about his next turn at the plate. He's due up next inning. It barely registers to him that Finkel is a left-handed batter.

Defense has never been important to Tyler, just a part of the game that he never gave much attention. Still, Tyler would admit, right field is nice and quiet; you can go games without being bothered by the ball, and that was all good with Tyler Weinberg. Moreover, it was a key component of Coach Reid's defensive strategy: Hide Weinberg, and hope they don't hit it to Wong.

You aren't supposed to think about hitting when you are in the field. Every coach says that. But hitting is *all* that Tyler thinks about. What else is there? So he stands in right field like a cow in a pasture, the bovine pleasure of his teeth gnashing a stick of chewing gum, thinking about his batting

81

stance. Tyler tells himself, *See the ball, hit the ball. See the ball, hit the ball.*

Deep in this meditation, it comes as something of a surprise to Tyler when he sees the ball—the actual ball, that famed product made in China with precisely 108 hand-sewn stitches—climbing into the sky and, *how now, brown cow,* coming in his direction.

Tyler sticks out his hand and the ball finds his glove. The runner on first, Nick Clemente, had gone more than halfway to second base. He is surprised to see the ball caught, and in such cavalier fashion; Clemente scurries back to first base, muttering words one should never say in church.

Wow, that was some grab by Tyler Weinberg, who is not known for his defense (cough, cough). That's two outs in the bottom of the fourth, the score still holds at one to nothing. Travis Green steps to the plate. Travis doubled his first time up....

Seven more outs, Dylan counts down. He's rolling now, it feels like he's getting stronger as the game goes on. Dylan stands on the rubber, peers in for the sign. His friend Travis Green wants to ruin Dylan's fine day. Last time up, Travis took their friendship a little too far—all the way to the wall, in fact. Dylan can't afford to let up on him again. Neither boy acknowledges the other. The game has turned serious; all friendships have been suspended until further notice.

Travis fouls off two pitches. Dylan's control is excellent.

Finally, the ball is at his command. Branden sets the target and Dylan hits the spot. He throws a pitch outside, trying to make Travis chase a bad one. He doesn't. The count runs to 1–2. Dylan comes back inside and gets Travis to bounce weakly to the second baseman, Patrick Wong.

Patrick waits for the ball and watches in mute agony as it rolls between his legs. Right through the wickets. Clemente races all the way to third. Travis reaches first on the error.

Dylan can't even look at Patrick. You can't make that kind of mistake in a one-run game. Not when it's for the championship. He stands behind the mound, rubbing the ball in his hands.

"Forget that play, make the next one!" Coach Reid yells to the infield. "Don't worry about it, Patrick. We'll get the next guy."

Now batting with runners on the corners, two outs, Marty Carbinowski. . . .

Sam figures that Carbinowski will not pose much of a problem for Dylan. Carbinowski is an oafish kid with feet that look like small gondolas. Tall and awkward, he's a little overweight with a soft body. Carbinowski has a thick head of curly red hair, an auburn tumbleweed that sticks out in peculiar ways beneath his helmet. There is nothing about him that says, "athlete."

The bigger concern, Sam thinks, is a wild pitch. Dylan has already bounced a few in the dirt today. But now with

Clemente on third, a wild pitch would mean a tie game. *Just fastballs*, Sam whispers to himself. *Stay away from the curve.*

Dylan blows the first pitch by Carbinowski for a strike. The big lug looks overmatched. His swing is wild and loopy. So Dylan goes after the hitter with another fastball.

It should have been a ball. The pitch is high, up in Carbinowski's eyes. A more disciplined hitter lays off that pitch. But Carbinowski swings and gets all of it. Dylan knows it is gone the moment the ball leaves the bat. The ball travels in a high-soaring arc, baseball's most sublime trajectory. It clears the center-field fence by fifteen feet.

A three-run homer, just like that.

Like a hatchet to Dylan's skull.

Sam Reiser watches in absolute shock. With one thunderous swat from the unlikeliest of sources, Northeast takes a 3–1 lead. The joyous team pours out of the dugout, waiting in a bouncing, bubbling throng for Marty Carbinowski—of all people!—to round the bases and step on home. *What a shot! The big ape finally got ahold of one!*

Catcher Branden Reid doesn't move. Not a muscle. Never gets up from his crouch. He holds his position, while all around him the Northeast players whoop and dance, push and crowd. Finally Branden stands, unfolds his lank limbs, and ambles out to the mound.

"Well, that definitely blows," he comments.

Dylan shakes his head, stunned. One minute he was cruising along with a shutout, the next minute it all goes up in smoke.

Branden watches Northeast celebrate. "What do they think? The game's over?" he complains. "It's only the fourth inning, Dill. Tell you what. Let's get this next guy. Then we go into the dugout, grab our bats, and get those runs back."

Patrick Wong picks up a stone from the infield dirt, flicks it aside, sickened. It was his error that prolonged the inning. *Why am I even here?* he wonders. Patrick had prayed that he wouldn't do something horrible on this day. Not in the championship game. Now Patrick realizes why Jasper Mednick didn't show for today's game. Mednick wasn't sick; he just didn't want to risk the humiliation. The pain of letting the team down.

Patrick thought back on the season, like leafing through a scrapbook of past failures. He struck out all the time. And while Patrick never dropped any fly balls, he couldn't remember catching any, either. Coach Reid tried him in a few different positions, trying to find a place, Patrick assumed, where he'd do the least harm. Right field, left field. Recently, he played a lot of second base. Got lucky on a few ground balls that bumped off his chest, his shins, and once, spectacularly, his cup. *Thwup, ooomph.* That'll wake you up.

It was true.

He was Mednick.

Or at least his team's version of Mednick.

He really did suck socks.

After today, I'll never play again, Patrick promises himself. *Never.*

Alex Lionni pounds a fist into his glove. Carter Harris chews the inside of his cheek. Nando Sanchez looks stunned, still facing home, hands on his knees, waiting for the next pitch.

In center field, Colin Sweeney watches as three neighborhood boys bound into the bushes after the home run ball. He remembers a line from *Bull Durham*. The catcher, Crash Davis, says it to the pitcher after an opponent hit a long home run: "Anything travels that far oughta have a stewardess on it."

Funny line.

That's the good thing about busy parents. They let you watch anything. Man, Colin loved movies. Things always turned out right in a movie. The good guys always won. Then he remembered *The Bad News Bears*. They lost that one, didn't they? Somebody—Kelly Leak? or was it the fat, curly-haired kid, Engelberg?—gets tagged out at the plate. The Bears lost. Somehow that made the movie even better. As if losing wasn't the end of the world. Colin supposed that was the message. You could lose and still be a winner.

What a bunch of hooey. You lose and they don't make movies about you, that's for sure.

Northeast now leads by a score of three to one. And second-sacker Billy Thompson steps to the plate. . . .

Somehow Dylan gets through it, enticing Thompson to bounce to short. As usual, Carter plays it like a song. The fourth frame is in the books. The Earl Grubb's team jogs off the field, disbelief etched on their faces.

· 9 ·

Top of the Fifth

	1	2	3	4	5	6	R	H	E
VISITORS	0	0	1	0	-		1	2	1
HOME	0	0	0	3			3	4	1

Coach Reid watches his team come off the field and he doesn't like what he sees. Heads are down, shoulders sagged. Their body language is all wrong.

He knows he has to kick-start this team right now—right this minute—or they might not recover.

"Gather round, right here, hustle up," he calls. "Come on, Carter, Dylan, Patrick, get in close, everybody."

Twelve boys and Coach Reid huddle in front of the dugout. Mr. Lionni and Coach Van Zant stand nearby, leaning in, listening to every word.

"We're only down two runs," Coach Reid says. "Just play the game, one pitch at a time. Give me some quality at-bats."

He turns to Dylan. "Hands together now, everybody on three: *team*. Dill, start us off."

At the top of his lungs, Dylan looks to the sky and hollers, "One-two-three!"

"TEAM!" the boys shout together.

"Excuse me, Jeff?" Mr. Lionni says.

"What?" Coach Reid looks at Casper Lionni, who is anxiously tapping the scorecard with a precisely sharpened, number-2 pencil.

"It's the fifth inning, Jeff. We have to make changes."

"Oh . . . shoot," Coach Reid says. "Let me see that book."

He confers briefly with Andy and decides how to handle the season's final two innings. "Bring in Max for Nando . . . Scooter for Alex . . . and, um . . . who else we got? Mike in for . . ." He glances at Branden, hesitates, seems to reject the idea. ". . . in for . . . Eamon."

"Got it. Young, Wells, and Tyree are in; Sanchez, Lionni, and Eamon Sweeney are out," Mr. Lionni confirms.

"We'll put Max behind the plate, and move Branden somewhere. I don't know where right now," Coach Reid says, head pounding.

"First base?" Casper Lionni suggests.

Coach Reid looks at Mr. Lionni with genuine surprise. He smiles. "Yeah, first base. Good idea."

"Are you keeping Dylan on the mound?" Andy asks.

"What?! Um, what do you think?"

"You're the manager, Jeff, that's why they pay you the big bucks," Andy Van Zant answers. He pauses. "But if you are asking my opinion, I'd stick with him."

"Okay, done," Jeff decides.

The lineups for the fifth and sixth innings now read:

• VISITORS •

Earl Grubb's Pool Supplies

PLAYERS	Pos.
Dylan Van Zant	P
Max Young	C
Branden Reid	1B
Carter Harris	SS
Mike Tyree	3B
Colin Sweeney	RF
Tyler Weinberg	LF
Patrick Wong	2B
Scooter Wells	CF

Northeast Gas & Electric

PLAYERS	Pos.
Justin Pinkney	SS
Frank Ausanio	CF
Angel Tatis	3B
Nick Clemente	P
Luther Dross	RF
Steven Smith	LF
Travis Green	C
Marty Carbinowski	1B
Joey Crocker	2B

Coach Van Zant claps his hands. "Boys, boys," he announces. "We've got The Wrong Sweeney leading off. Followed by Weinberg, followed by Wong—with Wells in the hole. My goodness, that's a lot of Ws."

Colin says with an Elmer Fudd-inspired lisp, "Sounds wike a wun to me, you wascally wabbits!"

It works; the boys laugh.

Upstairs, Sam Reiser puts a slash through the names on the official scorecard. He neatly pencils in the substitutions. He notes that only three Earl Grubb's players will be on the field for the entire game: Reid, Van Zant, and Harris. Two of them are coach's sons, of course. That's the way it is in Little League, everybody knows it. Sam surveys the field, there's Colin Sweeney swinging a bat in the on-deck circle. For that one single moment, Sam feels a powerful urge to leave. Just stand up, turn his back on the game, and walk away.

Why does it matter? Why do I care so much?

Sam knows he isn't going to grow up to become a big-leaguer. But even so, he feels an incredible burning in his body, a longing; he aches to play. Sam can close his eyes and see it. Stepping up to the plate, letting his eyes drift over the field, gradually picking up the pitcher. A practice swing, another, then bat back and ready. Hands at the shoulder, a little higher, elbows pointed down the way he prefers. A line-drive hitter, not a power guy. Just get the barrel on the ball and run like crazy. Here's the pitch and there it is, that sweet swing, and the ball jumps off his bat, a rocket over the shortstop's head and into the gap. He sees himself running fast out of the box, instantly thinking double, hoping triple, pulse pounding, stride strong, heart glad: You can live a lifetime and not hit too many like that, so cherish the moment.

All he wants is to feel it one more time.

Just like the other kids.

Robbed from me, he thinks.

Stupid *osteosarcoma*.

Boy. Doctors and their words.

Just a word, sure. Osteosarcoma. But a word that changed Sam's life.

When he first heard it, Sam was with his parents in Doctor Shrivastava's office. They sat across from her desk in three chairs, Sam feeling uncomfortable with his leg in a full splint. For some reason, the doctors didn't want his broken leg in a cast. They wanted *access*, they said, whatever that meant. The mood was serious, the small talk forced. Sam sensed that something of great significance was taking place. Like in church or something. The way his father sat so still, the way he leaned forward as if listening with his entire body. Sam's mother held a pen, a yellow legal pad on her lap. She was already taking notes. She had chittered nervously during the ride to the hospital, bizarrely upbeat, but now she had quieted, her thoughts turned inward.

Doctor Shrivastava greeted them, gestured to the chairs, smiled warmly, and it began. Sam's new life.

She wore an ID badge around her neck: *Doctor Amala Shrivastava, Pediatric Oncology*. She was going to give them answers. And the answer, it seemed, was osteosarcoma. Sam concentrated hard, trying to understand. It was the word that explained everything. All the things that had gone wrong. Why his leg broke so easily from a simple fall, the follow-up tests, the thing they found growing in his bone. The tumor.

And now they gave it a name. Sam had osteosarcoma. Or, well, osteosarcoma had him. The two words—Sam and osteosarcoma—were joined now, entangled, entwined, forever linked. Buried inside the big word, he discovered the letters to his own name, s-a-m. It was there all along.

Doctor Shrivastava looked from one to the other: Sam, his father, his mother. Mostly though, and to her great credit, the raven-haired doctor with milk-chocolate skin spoke directly to Sam, kept meeting his eyes, looking at him with sharp-eyed clarity and infinite kindness. She was nice. There was goodness in her, Sam felt it.

So. That was that. But what did it mean? It was as if doctors spoke only secret words no one could understand: *biopsy, retinoblastoma, metastasize, limb salvage,* and *chemotherapy*. Somehow all those words were stuck into Sam like darts, but they didn't seem real. All Sam really knew, judging from the way his mother kept chewing her lower lip, the way his father reached for Sam's hand and squeezed, was this: *Not good.*

Sam's mother kept scribbling on the legal pad, flipping pages, writing furiously. In Sam's family, she was in charge of facts. For reasons no one could explain, Sam had contracted the most common type of bone cancer. It usually appeared in teen boys, often during growth spurts. A tumor grew in Sam's leg. Doctor Shrivastava wanted to remove the bone before the cancer could spread. She said that they would replace the bone with a metal rod.

How weird was that?

This surgery, she said, would take place in about twelve weeks. During that time, and for nine months afterward, Sam would have to take some very strong medicine. The medicine, or chemotherapy treatment, would destroy the bad cancer cells in his body—but they would also make him feel very sick sometimes.

At a certain point, Sam stopped listening. He closed his eyes. It was dark, and he was swirling in an inky sea of words, drowning in the dark, mystic language. He needed to get away. Fly to some other place. He was tired of listening, tired of hushed conversations, of doctors and their white coats.

Dr. Shrivastava looked at Sam. "Most patients fully recover," she assured him.

Sam stifled a yawn. He had been stuck in this office forever.

"Can we go now?" he asked his parents.

"Sam? What?"

"I want to go to Mike's house," he announced. "He just got the new MLB game on PlayStation. He says it's awesome."

"Mike's house?" his mother repeated. "Sam, I . . . ?"

"It should be fine," Dr. Shrivastava intervened, checking her wristwatch. "Perhaps that's enough for one day." She looked at Sam, smiled warmly. "Mike is your friend?"

Sam nodded, yes, of course. Mike was his friend.

"His family knows," Mr. Reiser spoke up. "They know why we are here. I'm sure they'd be happy to have Sam visit. Mike and Sam are very good friends."

Sam was relieved. He wanted to get out of the office. He needed air. But then a question came to him. "Will I go bald?" he asked.

"Yes," the doctor answered, "very likely you will. Most patients do during chemotherapy." She smiled at Sam. "Don't worry, your hair will grow back. But in the meantime, I'm glad to see that you like hats."

Sam instinctively touched his New York Mets baseball cap. "Will I be better in time to play baseball this season?"

94

Doctor Shrivastava looked to Mr. Reiser. Hadn't the boy been listening?

"Sam is a very talented, enthusiastic baseball player," Mr. Reiser explained. "The regular Little League season ends in June."

"Oh, I see," Dr. Shrivastava answered. The corners of her mouth tightened, turned downward. "I'm afraid not, Sam. Your body is sick—you have a very serious illness—and we must treat that cancer very aggressively, right away, to make you strong again. I want you to play baseball, Sam. And very likely you will again. But first, we must deal with this illness."

Sam believed her. Of course he wasn't going to die, he knew that. He didn't have to ask about that. Even so, the thought thrilled him a little. Surgery, a metal bone, no hair. It was cool in a way. A scary roller coaster, like that Aerosmith ride at Disney World. But at the same time, all Sam really wanted was to be normal. Just do the stuff he always did. He wanted to go back to the life he had before he heard the word *osteosarcoma*.

Sam looked to his parents. "So, like, now can I go to Mike's?"

Hey, Sam! Yoo-hoo!" Colin Sweeney shouts up to the booth. "You going to announce me or what? You know I like a big introduction!"

The cry snaps Sam out of his daydream. He fumbles with the microphone, leans in, says:

My bad, um, that's Colin Sweeney at the plate,
top of the fifth. . . .

Clemente comes inside with the first two pitches and falls behind 2–0.

Colin taps the next pitch to third. Tatis gloves it, but his throw to first is in the dirt. Carbinowski can't handle the short hop. The ball trickles away and Colin Sweeney is safe on the error, grinning ear to ear.

"What's up, Carbinowski?" Colin greets the first baseman. "Boy, I sure am glad you didn't catch that one. I'd love to chat with you, but I don't think I'll be hanging around for long."

Here's Tyler Weinberg, who ripped a shot to left last
time up. . . .

The next pitch bounces to the backstop and makes Colin prophetic. "See ya!" he calls to Carbinowski, and takes off for second on the wild pitch.

Tyler takes a murderous swing and hits a little nubber down the third-base line, fair by inches, a swinging bunt. Sweeney advances to third, Weinberg is aboard on first. That's baseball, a game of skill combined with a heavy dose of dumb luck. First time up, Tyler hits a laser to left field for an out; next time, he dribbles a squibbler and his batting average climbs.

The tone has changed once again. With two runners on, a new suspense creeps into the air, like in a paperback thriller when the injured hero sets off alone into a darkened warehouse. The people in the stands sit up a little straighter, watch a little closer. Sam feels it in his voice, too, a sense of anticipation.

Runners on the corners, nobody out. Now up, Patrick Wong. . . .

In the third-base coach's box, Jeff Reid has a decision to make. Should he put on the bunt, or do nothing and hope Patrick earns a walk? He gives Tyler the steal sign, then calls time to speak with Patrick.

"I need you to take the first pitch to give Tyler a chance to steal second," he instructs Patrick. The boy looks anxious, like a rabbit who has just seen the shadow of a hawk.

"Patrick," Coach Reid says, "you can hit this guy. But you have _got_ to swing the bat. You understand?"

Patrick nods unconvincingly.

"Don't help him out, though. Make him throw strikes."

Patrick Wong steps into the batter's box, unsure of the message. The pitch is a strike. Tyler races to second base. The catcher, Travis Green, fakes a throw to second, sees Colin leaning the wrong way, and fires to Tatis at third. Colin scrambles back in a cloud of dust. "Safe," the field umpire signals.

The count runs full, three balls and two strikes. The bat

has not left Patrick's shoulder. But he swings at the next pitch—Wong finally swings!—and gets a piece of it. Amazing. He stays alive. Foul ball, the count remains full.

The Earl Grubb's players chatter in approval. Clemente's next pitch looks low, but the umpire rings Patrick up for strike three.

Some fans crow in complaint over the umpire's eyesight.

"Come on, that was ball four!"

Head down, Patrick Wong slowly walks to the dugout. It requires great effort not to cry. Another strikeout in a lifetime of strikeouts. He should have stayed home.

One away, runners hold at second and third. Scooter Wells steps to the plate. . . .

"Watch for the passed ball," Coach Reid reminds Colin. "You aren't forced on a grounder, but go if it gets past the pitcher. Be ready to tag on a fly."

"Come on, kiiiiiiiid!"

It's Mike Tyree again, looking to pump up the volume.

"Drive 'em in, Scooter!"

Clemente is taking more time between pitches, working methodically. Scooter lays off a couple of close ones and works out a walk. A quality at-bat.

The bags are drunk.

Batting for the third time, Dylan Van Zant. He's one for two on the day. One out, bases loaded. . . .

The mood is tight, like an elastic cord about to snap. Dylan feels it, tries to fight back the anxiety.

The at-bat is over in four pitches: Ball one, ball two, ball three, ball four.

All the runners advance as Dylan takes first base, forcing in a run with his second RBI of the game. Colin Sweeney pauses before reaching home plate, leaps high and stomps on it with both feet. The Earl Grubb's bench explodes. The score is 3–2, and the bases are reloaded.

Coach Reid checks the runners. Great speed on second in Scooter Wells, who represents the go-ahead run. *If there's a chance*, Coach Reid tells himself, *I've got to send him.*

Now up, batting for the first time today, Max Young. . . .

The Northeast manager, Rocco Clemente, calls time. He walks to the hill to confer with his son.

During the pause, a familiar voice calls to Mike Tyree from behind the chain-link backstop. "Hey, Slugger."

Mike turns to see his sister, Candace, standing to the right of the dugout. She is tall and toned, a burnished beauty with a killer smile.

"Hey," Mike says. He is surprised to see her.

Candace tilts her chin to the scoreboard in right field. "Some game, huh? You bat yet?"

"I'm up after Carter, probably next inning."

"Get a hit," she says.

"Sure," Mike answers. He doesn't smile.

Candace looks at her little brother, feels the gulf that has grown between them. They used to be such good friends. She doesn't know how to make it better. "Look, Mike, I know you got dragged to a ton of my games," she begins. "Today is *your* day. I wanted to be here to watch *you* win the championship."

"Right," Mike says, giving nothing, not even willing to imagine such a thing. Instead, he dwells on all the times he's had to sit in the stands to watch her, Candace Tyree, his superstar sister.

Mike Tyree sat between his parents a few rows behind the team bench in the Glens Falls Civic Center. He watched as his sister, Candace, hit basket after basket, grabbed rebounds, blocked shots. He saw the look in his mother's eyes. The misty-eyed pride. Saw the way his father's chest seemed to expand, how he held his chin just a little higher. Heard how the crowd cheered.

Candace Tyree—"Candy" to her friends—came down with the rebound. In one fluid motion, she turned and fired an outlet pass to a streaking teammate on the wing. Running hard, Candy raced up the floor and received the ball at the top of the key. She dribbled once, twice, stutter-stepped, then drove into the lane. Candy stopped and popped an eight-foot jumper. Nothing but net.

The crowd erupted.

"MVP! MVP!" came a chorus of chants from the student section. And why not? With only two minutes to go, the outcome of the high school game was no longer in doubt. The Delmar team would soon be crowned sectional champs, led by the impressive Candace Tyree. Tall, silky, athletic, gorgeous: She had it all, including a full scholarship to play Division I basketball at Georgia Tech next year.

Mrs. William Tyree reached for her husband's hand and squeezed. That was their little girl out there. She was special, and there was no telling how far she might go. The fans were cheering for her, screaming her name: "CAN-DY, MVP! CAN-DY, MVP!"

And all Mike felt was invisible.

All he could think was: *I hate her, I hate her, I hate her.*

Think positive," Candace tells him. "I mean it, Mike. Only good thoughts, you hear me?"

Mike glances up at the booth behind home plate. He sees Sam behind the pane, staring down on him, watching. Their eyes seems to lock.

"Yeah, good thoughts," he repeats absently.

Clemente, the Northeast manager, returns to his dugout.

"Batter up," the umpire yells.

"I can't talk now," Mike tells Candace.

Her lips tighten. It's Candy's turn to say nothing, give nothing. She blinks away her disappointment, moves to leave.

Mike almost calls after her. He almost speaks, almost tells Candace that he's glad she came. That it *means* something to him. But Mike doesn't open his mouth. Doesn't say a word. He watches as she walks away. Thinking maybe he should have said something.

Max Young lingers outside the batter's box. He has lived this moment a thousand times in his head, belting Wiffle balls over the house, alone in his dreams. The bases loaded, his team down by a run. Max isn't nervous. He isn't worried. He faces the pitcher and thinks, *Max Young steps to the plate. . . .*

Max lashes a line-drive single to center field. Tyler Weinberg trots home easily from third, tying the score. The center fielder, Frank Ausanio, plays the hard-hit ball cleanly on one hop. Coach Reid windmills his arms, beseeching Scooter Wells to score.

"Go, go, go!" he screams.

Scooter cuts the inside corner of the third-base bag with his right foot. Arms pumping, he races for home.

Ausanio fires from shallow center, the ball skips once on the grass to catcher Travis Green.

"Hit it! Hit it! Slide!" a cacophony of voices cry.

Scooter slides. Green catches the ball and sweeps the tag across Scooter's cleats.

"Out!" the home-plate umpire yells.

In that instant, everything freezes, a DVD on pause, then explodes into action. Both teams, the fans, the coaches—shouting, cheering, hooting, protesting—every emotion galvanized at once, a kinetic charge of energy rising up through the five layers of the earth's atmosphere, their cries and dreams climbing from troposphere to exosphere, soaring into the velvet void of deepest space. A roar that happens on Little League fields every day, in every town, city, state, and country all over the world, from Logansport to Osaka, San Cristobal to Little Rock. The sound the game makes when it is played passionately, with young hearts.

When the dust clears, the score is knotted at three. Beaming, Max Young stands on second base. Dylan Van Zant idles on third, twirling his helmet, his fingers in the holes of the earflaps. He's feeling good. Tie game!

Alex Lionni is drawn to the action like a magnet. He finds himself standing outside the dugout beside his father. "It doesn't get any better than this," Alex says.

Mr. Lionni, dressed in pleated khaki shorts, a tucked-in polo shirt, black socks, and brown loafers, smiles. "I see what you mean," he replies.

Sam can hardly speak. What could he possibly say that wouldn't diminish what they all had just seen?

Wow . . . wow! A clutch hit by Max Young ties it up, and a spectacular throw by Frank Ausanio keeps it tied. There are two outs, runners on second and third, and Branden Reid is due up next.

Branden stands near the plate, swinging his bat, eager and ready to rip. The Northeast team, on the other hand, is a mass of conflicting emotions. Ausanio's miraculous throw to the

103

plate—and Green's beautiful sweep tag—were huge, dramatic, flawless. But Northeast lost the lead, Clemente no longer looks invincible, and the game appears to be slipping away.

Sam looks across the diamond and studies the Northeast manager, Mr. Clemente, who faces a tough decision. Should he stick with his starter? Or go to a reliever? The decision is made even harder when you realize, as Sam does, that the pitcher is also the manager's son. Those guys have to drive home together after the game.

After a pause, Rocco Clemente holds out a meaty fist for Nick to see. "Get tough," he barks.

He's sticking with Nick, Sam thinks. He understands the decision, yet feels it might be a mistake. The boys are no longer intimidated by Clemente's fastball. He's running out of gas. Branden is due for a hit. This could be the game right here. Even so, Sam reasons, Nick has earned this shot. He's probably the best player in the league. It seems only fair that Northeast Gas & Electric should win or lose with Nick Clemente on the mound.

Confidence shaken, with first base open, Clemente pitches carefully. The count runs full. Branden lines the next pitch into shortstop Justin Pinkney's glove for the third out. Branden is hitless in three trips to the plate.

Even so, the Earl Grubb's dugout is pulsing with electricity. They were losing and they answered with two runs of their own. The whole season had come down to one final game, and now that final game has been whittled down, out by out, to an inning and a half. Deadlocked at three.

Anybody's ballgame.

Bottom of the Fifth

	1	2	3	4	5	6	R	H	E
VISITORS	0	0	1	0	2		3	4	1
HOME	0	0	0	3	-		3	4	2

Sam checks the Northeast lineup as they head to the bottom of the fifth inning. Top of the order coming up: Pinkney, Ausanio, Tatis. In other words, *trouble*.

He does a double take when he spots Branden Reid take over at first base. Sam guesses that it makes sense if Branden's arm is hurting. As a first baseman, he won't need to throw. And there's no way you take a guy like Branden out of the game. Still, it's strange to see him anywhere but behind the plate. Sam notes that Max Young is wearing the catching gear. It gives him an uneasy feeling.

Justin Pinkney leads things off for Northeast here in the bottom of the fifth inning. . . .

Max talks it over with Dylan on the mound. While Max doesn't love catching, he's steady behind the plate. Strong-armed and mobile. They decide to go after Pinkney with junk.

Pinkney gets way out in front of a lollipop curve. He rips it absurdly foul. Fifty feet into the parking lot. A window shatters. A car alarm blares. A fan in the stands groans. Another says, "I told you not to park there." A smattering of laughter ripples through the crowd. Tragedy, the stuff of comedy.

Now he's set, Dylan thinks. He follows with a high fastball on the outside part of the plate. Justin swings late and lofts a harmless fly to right.

Colin Sweeney makes the catch while humming the theme song to *Mission Impossible*.

Frank Ausanio, who already has a hit and an outfield assist in today's game, steps up. . . .

For the second time today, the aggressive Ausanio swings at the first pitch. He pulls a ground ball down the line, where Mike Tyree mans the hot corner. Mike reflexively dives and catches the ball with a backhand stab. For Mike, that was the easy part, all instinct. The throw to first is the tough part, because he has time to think, time to mess it up. His throw to Branden is high and off-line, but the catcher-turned-first-baseman leaps high, whirls, and applies a tag to the hard-charging runner. Nice play.

Yes! Sam thinks. *Way to go, Mike.* He jots a quick notation in the scorebook, making a circle to indicate another strong defensive play.

Mike can't help but steal a glance at his parents in the stands. They are both clapping, cheering. Candace is next to them, a huge smile on her face.

"Web gem," Carter compliments Mike.

Mike shakes his head. "I almost threw it away."

Carter grins, holds up two fingers, and shouts, "Two away!" As if to say, *An out is an out.* Don't question the gods of baseball.

"You're on a roll, Dilly-Dill. You're flowing now, number twelve," comes a voice from the dugout. It's Alex. Even the scrubeenies feel involved in the game. Three boys are on the Earl Grubb's bench: Nando Sanchez, Eamon Sweeney, and Alex Lionni. Nando is young for a sixth-grader, so he has another year of baseball at this level left. But for Eamon and Alex, it's the end of their "major league" careers. Next year, they'll move up to Babe Ruth. The field will be bigger, with ninety-foot base paths. The distance between the mound and home will be farther. There will be leading, stealing, and, most probably, fewer teams, fewer players, and fewer games. The boys will be thirteen, fourteen, fifteen years old. Many won't make the jump to the next level. Too many other things to do.

This game today, for the championship, is likely the most important baseball game many of these boys will ever play. And they will remember it all their lives.

That was a sweet diving stop by Mike Tyree, with a great catch-and-tag by Branden Reid at first. Two away in the bottom of the fifth. Batting third, Angel Tatis, who has been held hitless in two trips. . . .

On an 0–2 count, Angel hits a line drive to the gap between center and left field. Scooter Wells hustles over, hat flying off as he runs, and cuts it off. Scooter fires into second base, holding Tatis to a long single.

The Earl Grubb's team is playing great defense, Sam observes in the booth. He's happy for them. Pleased to see Carter, Scooter, Dylan, and Mike play so well. He feels a knot of worry tighten in his stomach when the next batter heads to the plate.

Nick Clemente, he groans. The guy can mash. And the cell phone rings. *Not now.*

"Hello?"

It's Sam's father. He's at the game, waiting to give Sam a ride home when it's over. He wants to know, "Do you need anything? Something to drink or . . . ?"

Sam cuts him off. "I'm fine, Dad. I don't *need* anything. I gotta go."

He snaps the cell shut. After a pause, Sam announces the next batter.

Now batting, Nick Clemente. . . .

Clemente practically runs to the batter's box. He twirls his bat menacingly and scowls. Clemente has one singular intention: *to hit the ball a country mile.* He knows he can do it, too.

Max gives Dylan the target, low and inside. He wiggles an index finger. Fastball. Clemente takes it at the knees.

"Strike," the umpire calls.

Clemente snorts. "You're killing me, blue," he complains. Clemente steps out of the box, shakes his head in disbelief. He drives the next pitch into left field for a clean single. Angel Tatis, a fast runner, rounds second. When Tyler bobbles the ball, Tatis alertly takes off for third. Tyler doesn't seem to notice. He lobs the ball to Carter, who stands on the edge of the outfield grass, halfway between third and second. Tatis slides safely into third.

Carter runs the ball into the mound and calls, "Time."

The Northeast Gas & Electric dugout rattles and hums. Clemente, on first base, smashes his paws together in triumph. Angel Tatis brushes the dirt from his uniform.

"Waydahgo, waaaydahgo!" cheers the Gas & Electric bench.

That was Clemente's second hit of the afternoon. Is there anything he can't do? Once again today, the go-ahead run is on third base. Luther Dross steps to the plate.

Coach Reid walks out to the mound, waving the infielders in for a conference. "I don't think he's going to try to steal in this spot," Coach Reid says of Nick Clemente, who cools his heels on the first-base bag. "But if he goes, Max, I want you to zip it to Carter on the grass. Just like we've practiced. Carter, if Angel breaks for home, nail him at the plate."

"Sounds like a plan," Carter says. Like any good player, Carter wants the ball in a tight spot. Mike nods, Branden smacks Dylan on the butt. Only Patrick Wong stands motionless. He wishes he was on the bench. Or better yet, at home with his Xbox.

Luther Dross steps toward the plate. The crowd stirs in anticipation.

"Weak hitter, you struck him out last time," Coach Reid whispers to Dylan. "Don't fool around, no nibbling on the corners, go right after him."

Dylan blows two fastballs by Luther, who flails at both.

Max wiggles two fingers, calling for a curve. Dylan shakes him off. Max sends down one finger. Dylan nods, pulls down his cap, goes into the windup.

They say that even a blind squirrel will eventually find a nut. And even a dismal hitter, if he endeavors to swing, will sometimes put the bat on the ball. And to Patrick's abject horror, that same ball now bounces toward him, like a tiger that has identified its prey: Patrick Wong, the weakest gazelle in the herd.

Mike and Sam, best friends, do not need to lock eyes in this instance. But they do share the same thought: *Uh-oh*.

I'm dead meat, Patrick thinks.

Tatis breaks for home on contact. Moving from first to second, Clemente crosses in front of the ball, momentarily blocking Patrick's view. Luther Dross, sufficiently recovered from the shock of connecting with the pitch, motors toward the first-base bag.

Patrick fields it cleanly. He hesitates, uncertain now what to do with the round white rock. He looks toward second base.

"First base!" Carter yells, pointing.

Patrick turns, still holding the ball in his glove.

"Throw it!" Branden cries.

In the next moment, teammates are pounding Patrick Wong on the back. They are running off the field, smiling, giddy, intoxicated.

Patrick Wong made the play.

In the din and commotion, something makes Carter pull away from his teammates before entering the dugout. He hears a familiar whistle. Someone is calling his name. Carter looks to the grandstand. There's Uncle Jimmy, standing up, pointing at him, thumbs up.

Maybe, Carter thinks.

Maybe.

The thought is simple enough, yet to Carter it seems to offer an unimagined possibility. A new hope. Clear skies.

Hmmm, maybe.

Five innings have come and gone. The score is tied. And the game turns, like a great wheel, to the top of the sixth.

· 11 ·

Top of the Sixth

	1	2	3	4	5	6	R	H	E
VISITORS	0	0	1	0	2		3	4	1
HOME	0	0	0	3	0		3	6	2

This, folks, has been a tremendous game. We're in the top of the sixth inning. And now Earl Grubb's All-Star shortstop, Carter Harris, leads it off against Nick Clemente. . . .

As Carter steps to the plate, Colin Sweeney remembers a favorite line from *Jurassic Park*. It was said by Ray Arnold, the character played by Samuel L. Jackson (he also played Mace Windu in the *Star Wars* movies), right before he turns off the crippled park's power: "Hold on to your butts."

That cracks Colin up. Every time. Well, here they are, tied up in the sixth inning of the championship game. "Hold on to your butts, boys," Colin says in the dugout. And it gets a laugh from Nando, so Colin repeats the line, louder this time, "Hold on to your butts!"

Colin is due up third this inning, already has a bat in his hands, and he's repeating the line like a chant.

Tyler Weinberg hears him and obliges. He bends down, reaches behind him, and squeezes his cheeks.

"Aw, that's disgusting!" Scooter roars. He showers Tyler with a fistful of sunflower seeds.

Finally, Coach Van Zant pokes his head into the dugout. "Colin, boys, please!"

Colin nods, looks away, grins at Scooter. Coach Van Zant takes things too seriously.

At that exact moment, as Colin intones the word "butt"—his tongue pushing against the roof of his mouth to form the percussive double "tt"—Carter crushes a ball to the right-field corner. The relay throw is bungled and Carter coasts into third with a stand-up triple. The coolest play in baseball.

Uncle Jimmy whistles from the bleachers.

Carter gives a big, loud high-five to Coach Reid. *Smack.*

The place goes nuts.

Colin Sweeney knows that he's found the winning formula. The good-luck charm. As the next batter, Mike Tyree, consults with Coach Reid, Colin continues to direct a world of bad voodoo at the Northeast team. He repeats in a whisper, "Hold on to your butts. . . . Hold on to your butts. . . . Hold on to . . ."

*Batting for the first time today, hard-slugging
Mike Tyree. . . .*

Mike hears Sam's announcement and shakes his head in embarrassment.

"Come on, kiiiiiiiid!" roars Nando Sanchez, echoing Mike's signature phrase.

These little jokes relax Mike, help keep him calm.

"Play's at the plate!" Coach Clemente instructs his team. "Get tough, Nick. Throw hard."

Sam sees the Northeast infield creep in on the edge of the grass. Man on third, nobody out. He knows that the worst thing Mike can do in this situation is strike out. Carter can score on a sac fly, or even a ground ball. All Mike has to do is put the ball in play.

Come on, Mike, Sam whispers inaudibly. *This is your chance, you can do it, come on. . . .*

On Clemente's first pitch, Mike rifles a clean single up the middle. Carter cruises home for the go-ahead run. The hit brings three fans to their feet. Mike's parents and sister, Candace, stomp and whoop in appreciation. Mike can't help but grin ear to ear. His eyes lift toward the booth, where he can make out Sam behind the glass. He thinks he sees a raised fist, or maybe that's just a trick of the light.

*That was a clutch piece of hitting from Mike
Tyree! Earl Grubb's takes the lead here in the sixth
inning. Colin Sweeney steps to the plate. . . .*

Hold on to your butts. . . . Hold on to your butts, Colin repeats under his breath.

"Excuse me?" the umpire asks.

"What?"

"Did you say something?"

Colin laughs, shakes his head. "Just talking to myself."

Everyone in the Earl Grubb's dugout is pumped. The boys resemble monkeys in a zoo, scrambling around, bouncing, jostling, climbing, chattering, screeching. Everyone cheers encouragement.

"Let's go, Colin!"

"Come on, kiiiiiiid!"

"You can do it!"

Everyone, that is, except for Eamon, who watches his mirrored twin—The Wrong Sweeney—in measured stillness. Eamon stands in his favorite spot, the near corner of the dugout, closest to home plate. He leans against the mesh, watches, and listens. Finally the words come to him. The right words for his twin.

Eamon hollers, "Have fun!"

He had heard those words before, countless times, but never gave them much attention. Having fun was his brother Colin's department. Eamon took things more seriously. He recalls when he heard those words most recently. And this time he gets it. He absolutely, positively gets it. Fun, right? That's the idea—because life isn't always that way.

Before the game, Eamon must have been the most nervous kid on the team. For some reason, the "big game" had become, for him, the biggest burden in the world. Eamon was weighed down with worries. Ninety-six pounds of stress. Eamon had taken his customary spot in the corner of the dugout. He was a listener, a dedicated eavesdropper, and when Eamon pressed against the protective mesh, he could see his three coaches as they stood talking by the side of the dugout. Mr. Lionni had missed Coach Reid's pregame comments, so he asked, "Any great words of wisdom?"

Coach Reid seemed embarrassed. "I don't know. What did you think, Andy?"

"You did good," Mr. Van Zant replied. "I was worried for a minute you were going to give the old Jimmy Valvano speech."

"Ha!" Coach Reid hooted.

"The . . . *what?*" Mr. Lionni asked.

"Jimmy Valvano," Coach Van Zant said. "He was a great college basketball coach who died of cancer. A wonderful spirit. Anyway, Valvano gave a famous speech at the ESPY Awards toward the end of his life. . . ."

" '*Don't give up, don't ever give up!*' " Coach Reid said, echoing Valvano's famous words. "Man, I'll never forget watching that speech on TV."

"I look it up on the Internet every couple of years," Mr. Van Zant said. "Chokes me up every time."

Listening, Eamon made a mental note: *Jimmy Valvano, ESPY Awards, Internet.* He'd Google it when he got home. He thought of Sam Reiser up there in the booth. People die from cancer. Eamon knew that. But could it happen to a kid in his social studies class? A friend? No, Sam was doing all right.

Eamon realized how much he liked hearing Sam announce the games, just his voice, and how that made everything seem normal, gave everybody the feeling that it would be okay. That was like Sam's gift to everybody. No matter how sick he felt, he kept showing up at the games. It was his way of saying, *It's gonna be all right.*

Eamon listened again to the men's laughter. "So what *did* you tell them?" Mr. Lionni asked.

Coach Reid grinned. "Have fun."

"That's it?"

"Basically, yeah. That's the best I could come up with. 'Play hard, do your best, have fun.' Not so great, right?"

Mr. Lionni put his hand on Coach Reid's shoulder. "Actually, Jeff," he said, "I think it was perfect."

Eamon Sweeney agreed.

On the mound, however, Nick Clemente is decidedly not having fun. None whatsoever. His team is losing 4–3. There's a runner on first base, nobody out. Nick's job is to limit the damage. Somehow he's got to survive this inning without surrendering another run. Keep the game close.

Colin taps a slow bouncer to third baseman Angel Tatis. The ball is hit too softly for a force at second base, but Angel fires to first to nip the hard-running Sweeney.

One away. Tyler Weinberg is the batter. . . .

Red Bull swaggers purposefully to the batter's box. He doesn't check for the coach's signs, doesn't linger for any practice swings. He is solely focused on Nick Clemente, eager for the white ball to come his way. His mind is clear, uncluttered. See ball, hit ball. The world is his piñata.

Ty-Ty smash.

Clemente misses the first two pitches badly, up and away. Tyler fears one thing only: He doesn't want to walk. Not today, not in the sixth inning of the last game. The next pitch is high, in his eyes, so Tyler tomahawks the ball and sends it crashing against the left-field fence. Mike Tyree races home and Tyler reaches second with a double. The score is 5–3, Earl Grubb's over Northeast.

"Time!"

Rocco Clemente hurries to the mound. The father and son talk things over. The father turns and leaves, the son remains on the mound.

That was some shot by Tyler Weinberg, one of the hitting stars of the day. Up next, Patrick Wong....

There's a scene in the movie *The Matrix* where a boy stares at a spoon and the metal object melts like hot rubber. It's a neat trick. He bends it with his mind.

This is what Patrick Wong thinks about when he's at the plate. He will not swing. Instead, all of his focus is on Nick Clemente. By sheer concentration, Patrick hopes to *will* the ball out of the strike zone. He wants to create an invisible shield around home plate, like Sue Storm of the Fantastic Four, forcing the ball out of the strike zone.

"Just throw strikes," Rocco Clemente barks after Nick misses with the first two pitches.

Patrick smiles secretly. *It's working.*

The count runs full.

"Careful now, Patrick," Coach Reid murmurs. He, too, is hoping for a walk.

Nick Clemente's final pitch of the day cuts the inside corner at the knees. A perfect fastball on the black. The umpire rises from his crouch, gestures to first. "Ball four."

Patrick hurls his bat toward the dugout and flies to first base on a magic carpet. *It works*, he thinks. *I did it! I have superpowers!*

Nick Clemente is beside himself. The burly hurler stomps and groans in despair. Rocco Clemente rushes to the mound, takes the ball from his son, puts a hand on his shoulder. Nick pulls away.

Sam Reiser watches as Nick Clemente, the biggest kid on the field, seems to shrink before his eyes. Head bowed, eyes on the ground, the boy listens as his father talks. He turns and walks to his new position in center field. Frank Ausanio trots in from center, passing Clemente on the way. Neither appears to say a word.

Everyone in the Earl Grubb's dugout watches this pantomime. They feel one thing: *Triumph.* They just knocked the best pitcher in the league out of the box. Best of all, it was Patrick Wong who did it, he was the straw that broke the camel's back.

> *Here comes Frank Ausanio in to pitch, with Nick Clemente moving to center field. Hey, that was some great performance by Clemente. . . .*

On cue, the fans offer a round of cheers for the Northeast pitcher.

> *Scooter Wells is due up next. Runners at first and second, still only one man down. . . .*

As Ausanio warms up—he throws with a herky-jerky motion, but appears to have little idea of where the ball is going—Dylan Van Zant sidles up next to Scooter.

"He's wild," Dylan notes.

"This is my last at-bat," Scooter says, staring straight ahead.

Dylan doesn't understand at first. "This season? Or you mean . . . ?"

"I'm done after this year."

"Why?" Dylan asks. "You're a great player."

Scooter shrugs. "I guess I'm more into skateboarding, mountain biking, hanging out, being with my friends."

Dylan smiles. "Oh, you mean like . . . Sophia?"

Scooter laughs. Yes, girls were most definitely a part of the equation. But the truth was, most of his friends didn't play baseball. Scooter's heart just wasn't in it anymore.

Ausanio finishes his warm-ups.

Scooter Wells, in his final Little League at-bat, proceeds to walk on five pitches.

Again, the bases are loaded. A hit here will break the game open.

Dylan Van Zant, already with two RBIs on the day, comes to bat with three ducks on the pond. . . .

Ausanio misses with the first pitch, then throws a "get me over" fastball. Dylan's eyes almost pop out of his head, but the lefty swinger is out in front of the pitch. He lofts the ball to medium right field.

"Tag, tag!" Coach Reid yells to Tyler.

Tyler scrambles back to the bag, waits for Luther Dross to make the catch in right, and sprints home to beat the throw. The base runners advance on the throw to the plate: Wong to third, Wells to second. The play isn't close, and suddenly, neither is the score. Earl Grubb's is up, 6–3. The team, the coaches, the parents can all feel it. This is their game now. This is their time.

They are going to win.

Max Young tied the game in the fifth with a big two-out single. Now he bats again, this time with two runners in scoring position. . . .

Coach Clemente signals for Ausanio to intentionally walk Max Young. He loads the bases to set up the force at any base. Textbook baseball.

Max accepts the walk with resignation, tosses his bat aside, and makes a quick comment to a teammate before hustling down the line. Max tells Branden, "Make 'em pay."

Now batting, Branden Reid. . . .

Sam notes that Branden has gone 0–3 on the day. He wonders if Branden has ever gone hitless in four at-bats. Well, there's always a first time. Because Branden whiffs on three pitches, the last one a curveball that bounces a foot before the plate. Just awful.

"That's okay!" Coach Reid hollers, clapping his hands. "Great job, boys, great job! Three more outs. Stay focused. One pitch at a time."

The boys charge onto the field as if they were led by Lawrence of Arabia. All except for Dylan, who walks to the mound, head down, lost in thought. There's an uneasy feeling in his stomach. Nerves. For the first time all day, now that he's on the brink of victory, Dylan is scared.

Scared of blowing it.

· 12 ·

Bottom of the Sixth

	1	2	3	4	5	6	R	H	E
VISITORS	O	O	1	O	2	3	6	7	1
HOME	O	O	O	3	O	-	3	6	2

We go now to the bottom of the sixth inning, last licks for Northeast Gas and Electric. They need three runs to tie. Steven Smith leads it off....

Dylan remembers Smith from his previous at-bat. He looked bad on a curveball. Not an impressive hitter. Dylan gets ahead in the count with fastballs, then finishes Smith with a curveball, low and away.

Now it's Travis Green's turn. He's already doubled and scored a run today....

Two more outs, Sam thinks, *and this game's history.* He reaches for the scorebook, marks a "K" for Smith's strikeout in the appropriate column. He flips the book over to tabulate the box score for the Earl Grubb's players. To Sam, it really is like a book he can read, except the language is baseball with symbols like "6–3" and "K" and "BB." He could look at the page and read the story, chapter by chapter, re-creating the game's events in his mind.

Sam quickly does the math. Dylan Van Zant had a great day with three runs batted in, not to mention that he was almost certainly going to be the winning pitcher. Carter Harris had only one hit, but it was a huge one, a triple to lead off the sixth. Branden Reid did nothing. Tyler Weinberg had two hits on the day, scored twice. Mike Tyree got a bad break with only one chance at the plate. But boy, did Mike make it count, a single to score Carter to break the tie.

Engrossed in the scorebook, Sam barely notices when Dylan falls behind in the count 2–0, the second pitch skipping to the backstop.

The voices begin drumming in Dylan's head:

"Nice and easy, Dill!"

"Pitch and catch, pitch and catch!"

His father calls, "Just throw strikes."

Though he's heard it a thousand times, this time the advice irritates the slender southpaw. Dylan steps off the mound, glares at the dugout. He thinks, *Gee, what an idea. Throw strikes—why didn't I think of that?*

The next pitch just misses, and the pitch after that misses by more than "just."

Travis Green gallops to first base. He claps his hands and hollers, "Okay, Marty. Do it again."

Sam tells the crowd:

Here's Marty Carbinowski. Marty hit that three-run bomb back in the fourth. . . .

"Just throw strikes, Dylan."

"Come on, number twelve."

"Dig deep, Dill. Don't give in."

The count runs to three balls and a strike. Dylan is feeling fatigued, bouncing pitches in the dirt. His legs feel tight, heavy as sandbags. He can't seem to get any "push" off the rubber, no drive forward. But mostly, it is Dylan's brain that's fried.

Carbinowski drills a flat fastball through the hole between Reid and Wong for a single. The lead base runner, Travis Green, reaches second base and holds. Down by three runs, Travis is too smart to take unnecessary chances. It is not worth it to risk getting thrown out at third base in that situation.

Coach Reid requests "time" and walks to the mound. The entire infield gathers around.

"Look," Coach Reid says. "We are up by three runs. These base runners don't matter. Don't worry about them. Just get the sure out."

Branden pounds a fist into his glove.

"Are you okay?" Reid asks Dylan.

"A little tired," the pitcher admits.

"Two more outs, Dill. Reach back. One pitch at a time. Stay focused. Just you and the glove."

Dylan steps off the mound to spit, but nothing comes. His mouth is too dry.

Upstairs, Sam writes in the scorebook. The game has suddenly gotten tense again. A home run would tie it. Crocker is up, he's not great, but then it goes to the top of the order: Pinkney, Ausanio, Tatis . . . and Clemente.

You never know.

That was another huge hit from Marty Carbinowski, who has really come up big today for Northeast. Runners at first and second, one out. Joey Crocker bats for the second time today. . . .

Dylan paces behind the mound, exhales, inhales. Crocker is a spindly speedster, a hyper kid who chokes up, crouches low, and runs like the wind. He's not a home-run hitter, but he's definitely a pain in the . . . er, *neck*.

Dylan throws a fastball for strike one. Crocker is taking all the way. The next fastball is far outside, but Max Young manages to get his glove on it. Dylan bounces the next pitch. Again, Max makes a good play.

I'm cooked, Dylan realizes. He rolls his eyes skyward: No help there.

Coach Reid nervously fingers a paper clip, twisting it into

a mangled shape. "Come on, Dylan!" he calls. Thinking, *Just get this one guy.*

Joey Crocker lashes a single to center. Travis Green scores, Marty Carbinowski rumbles to second, Crocker is safe on first with an RBI single.

Sam's eyes widen, he sits up straight. *Oh my God*, he murmurs, *they could blow this.*

The score is now 6–4. The tying run stands on first base in the fleet personage of Joey Crocker, 180 feet and two left turns from home.

Again, the umpire grants "time" to Coach Reid. It's his second visit to the mound this inning, making for an automatic pitching change.

Coach Reid heads to the mound, glances at Carter at short, then decides. His head swivels to Max Young. "Take off the gear, Max. I'm going with you."

Max stands on the grass, halfway between home and the pitcher's mound. "Now . . . ?"

"You're pitching, Max," Coach Reid says.

"Right, okay, right," Max stammers. He did not see this coming.

Coach Reid takes the ball from Dylan. "You've pitched a great game, Dill," he says. "Now I need you to play first base."

"But I'm only two outs away," Dylan protests. "I can finish this."

"First base," Coach Reid repeats. He turns to his son. "Branden, put on the gear."

Branden leans into his father and whispers, "I can't throw, Dad."

"I don't want you to throw," the father replies. "I want you to think. I need your brains back there, Branden. I don't care if you have to roll the ball back to the pitcher like it's the Pro Bowlers Tour."

Okay, um, looks like we've got a pitching change. Max Young takes the hill, Dylan Van Zant slides over to first base, and Branden Reid is back behind the plate. . . .

While Max takes his warm-ups, Coach Reid returns to stand between Andy Van Zant and Casper Lionni.

"Do either of you guys know CPR?" he jokes. "Because I think I'm going to have a heart attack."

It's a funny moment, but no one laughs. The game has taken on a new tension, like a coiled rope, twisting tighter and tighter. Everyone feels it, perhaps the coaches most of all. For the Northeast team, they are filled with new hope and excitement. The game had looked lost—the season over—and now, suddenly, they are back in it. The pressure has shifted squarely to Earl Grubb's Pool Supplies. They have everything to lose. And each boy feels the strain.

Justin Pinkney is due up next. Then Frank Ausanio. The Northeast team has a shot, a real shot. They all watch Max Young. A smooth delivery, but he doesn't throw very hard. Besides, he's a righty. They are glad to have seen the last of the southpaw, Van Zant. Collectively, watching Max they reach the same conclusion: *Hittable.*

The relief pitcher, Max Young, is not nervous. He has been in spots like this hundreds of times before . . . with one important difference. It was never the real thing.

For years, Max stepped into his backyard, walked off the proper distance from his pitchback, and entered the limitless realm of his imagination. He played fantasy games on his very own field of dreams. And all the while, Max talked to himself, taking on the voice of the radio sportscaster. Somehow the words made it real. In a barely audible whisper he'd murmur: "*Leading off for the Legends team, it's Tyrus Raymond Cobb. The Georgia Peach led the American League in batting eleven times for a career .367 average. . . . Here comes the pitch . . . and it's a swing and a miss. . . . Got 'em with the heater. . . . Cobb glares at the pitcher, Max Young. . . .*"

And so it would go, Max Young battling against the all-time greats. Some days he would pull out a notebook and face classic teams, such as the 1998 New York Yankees, the 1934 St. Louis Cardinals, and the 1975 Cincinnati Reds. Max knew all their names and lineups. Most of all, he knew the numbers. Batting averages, RBI totals, home runs, stolen bases. Max could recite statistics to the decimal point. He knew the numbers by heart, and the expression was only too true; for it was as if his heart, and not his brain, stored the information.

Ted Williams hit .406 in 1941.

In 1982, Rickey Henderson stole 130 bases for the Oakland Athletics.

Cy Young notched 511 career wins.

Max Young loved baseball. And baseball loved him back. He felt it from the soles of his cleats to the top of his cap.

"Batter up!" the umpire calls.

The stands stir, a few parents call out encouragement. But most sit in silence, chewing fingernails.

Max Young receives the sign from Branden. One finger, a fastball. Pinkney takes it for a strike. A good location, right on the outside corner. Max hits the same spot again, but this time Justin smacks a grounder toward the hole between first and second base.

Patrick Wong, the second baseman, has no chance. But Dylan, the newly installed first baseman, ranges into the hole and makes the grab. He looks to second base and Carter is there, straddling the bag, calling for the ball. Dylan throws a perfect strike to get the force.

Carter calls "time," walks the ball into Max Young. There are base runners at third and first. Two outs. Carter flips the ball to Max. "Get this guy and we all eat ice cream."

A sweet play by Dylan Van Zant at first base! He's done everything today. Northeast is down to their last out. Up comes tough Frank Ausanio. . . .

Sam notices himself rocking now, back and forth in his chair, his hands clenched in his lap. Ausanio is very strong, a rugged kid. He can end this game with one swing. It is killing Sam to sit and watch helplessly, much harder, he thinks, than to be down on the field. At least down there, he could *do* something.

If only I could play, he thinks. *If only I could be down there. If only.*

Sam stops himself mid-thought. He can't go down that road. Instead, he gives himself over to the game. All he can do is watch.

Max Young stands on the mound. He thinks, *Max Young looks in for the sign. Shakes off the curveball, nods, goes into the windup. . . .*

Ausanio blasts the pitch into left-center field. Carbinowski races home to bring the score to 6–5. Scooter Wells cuts the ball off before it rolls to the wall. He throws in to Carter, who spins, ball cocked by his ear. There's no play.

The Northeast team goes bananas.

"Wayduhgo . . . wayduhgooo . . . waaaaayduhgo!"

The boys are banging their bats against the bench, *boom, boom, boom!* They are wearing their caps inside out and backwards for good luck. Rally caps. And it seems like it's working.

Sam calculates the odds. Justin Pinkney stands on second base. He represents the tying run. Good speed, Justin can probably score on a single to the outfield. The potential go-ahead run, Ausanio is on first, totally amped. He holds up two fists to the next batter, Angel Tatis.

Angel nods and spits, twisting his hands on the bat handle.

And behind Angel, Nick Clemente awaits on deck. The masher. He's already banged out two hits today. Clemente longs for number three.

The score is six to five, folks. Northeast is one hit away from tying this game up. Now batting, Angel Tatis. Angel roped a single his last time up, he's one for three on the day. . . .

"Let's go, kiiiiiiiid!" screams Mike Tyree to Max from third base. Sam has to smile, watching Mike down on the field. He looks as nervous as a cat in a car wash. Mike blows into his glove, wipes his hand on his pants, backs up a step, glances to the runner on second, pounds a fist into his glove, jabbers to the pitcher in deathless monotone, "Come on, Max; come on, Max; come on, Max. . . . "

Baseball is a team game. But it is also a game that provides moments when a player must stand alone. Every batter experiences this, that time when no teammate can help you.

For a pitcher, the sense of isolation is even more profound. Alone on the mound, he is elevated ten inches above all others, a fool on a hill. It is only a pitcher who can be "given" the win or "take" the loss. *Max Young takes the loss. Max Young blows the save.* And so on.

No other position bears that responsibility.

It is a job for an egotist. And an optimist. No others need apply. Because if a pitcher loses his confidence, once doubt enters his mind, you might as well put a fork in him, he's done.

When the game is going well, a pitcher feels as if he's on top of the world, the king of the mountain. The spotlight is on him, shining brightly. But what blinding glare when he fails, a star crashing to earth. The humiliation is public for all to see. Max Young stands on the rubber, feeling the pressure. *The reality.* A crushing weight presses down on him, like a diver too far beneath the ocean's depths. He blinks once, twice, tries to focus. He feels utterly alone.

"You can do it, Max," Dylan calls from first base.

"Let's go, number six!"

Looking out from behind his mask, Branden doesn't like what he sees. Ausanio smoked that last pitch, and Max looks freaked.

"Time, blue," he calls.

Branden trots out to the mound. He takes off his mask, holds his glove near his mouth.

"See that old guy sitting near third base?" he whispers.

"What?"

"The guy with the straw hat? He has a blanket on his lap, looks about a hundred years old."

Max turns, notices the old man sitting on a lawn chair. "So?"

"That's Earl Grubb," Branden says.

"Who?"

"Earl Grubb . . . of Earl Grubb's Pool Supplies," Branden says. "He's the big kahuna."

"Really? That's him?"

Branden smiles; he can't keep up the ruse any longer. "Nah, I'm making that up. It's my grandfather."

Max stares blankly. "What? Earl Grubb is your grandfather?"

Branden laughs. "No, he's . . . never mind."

"But?"

"Listen to me, Max," Branden says, changing his tone, serious now. "Do *not* shake me off again. Got that? I put down a sign, you throw that pitch like you mean it."

Max nods.

"Trust me, okay? I know how to get this guy out. We'll get through this together. You hear me? Just believe."

"Just believe," Max repeats. He feels relief in the strength of Branden's certainty. His lungs fill with air. He can breathe again.

Branden hustles back behind the plate, chuckling to himself. Earl Grubb, that was a good one. Wait till he tells Grampa. Branden hopes that his visit jolted the jitters out of Max. It better have, he decides, or this game's toast.

Two fingers wiggle like worms. Max Young throws a curveball. Angel takes it high for a ball. Two fingers again. Angel swings and misses.

"Way to go, Max."

"Pitch and catch, pitch and catch!"

Carter glances into the stands. He catches Uncle Jimmy's eye. And there's his mom, right beside him. Carter pulls down his cap, grooms the infield dirt with his cleat, and waits. Carter thinks about poor Matty Alou, the dejected ballplayer in that old photograph of the San Francisco Giants. Baseball can be such a cruel game. Losses hurt so bad.

"Come on, Max," he suddenly barks with surprising fierceness. "Let's win it right here!"

Max throws a fastball. Angels fouls it back. Two strikes.

"One more, one more, one more," Dylan murmurs. Twenty feet to his right, Patrick Wong constructs an invisible force field around second base. He thinks, *Please, God in heaven, don't let them hit it to me.*

Branden puts down two fingers. He sets up outside, off the plate. He's calling for Max to throw a pitch outside the strike zone. He wants Angel to go fishing. Max throws, Angel holds, the count runs 2–2.

Branden lifts up his mask, spits with gusto. "I guess there's no time like the present," he whispers to himself. Branden puts down one finger. A fastball. He opens and closes his glove, holding it above his head.

Max takes the sign, nods, understands. *He wants me to climb the ladder.*

One last time, Max Young is alone in his daydreams, throwing against an imaginary hitter in a game of his own invention. He is the author and the instrument, the pitcher and the ball, the beginning and the end.

Max rocks back into his windup, he drives forward, the ball leaves his fingertips, comes in high and hard and true.

Angel Tatis hits nothing but air. Swing and a miss.

That's it. Game over.

Max flops to his knees, flings his glove high into the sky. All the boys rush the mound, shouting, screaming, piling on. In that instant, all the accumulated anxiety releases. And each boy on Earl Grubb's Pool Supplies becomes, for one single, shivery instant, forever bound together as a team. Each boy linked by that powerful emotion. *Champions*.

Patrick Wong hugs Nando Sanchez. Eamon Sweeney climbs to the top of the pile, hooting in elation. Tyler charges in from the outfield, diving into the mob like a mosh pit. Alex finds Dylan, puts his hands on his shoulders. "You're the winning pitcher, Dill. You did it! You won the championship game!"

Carter high-fives everyone in sight. He runs to the backstop, smiling up at his mother and Uncle Jimmy. Carter lifts a finger, one finger in the air. We're number one. Uncle Jimmy points down at him, beaming. "That's what I'm talking about, Carter!" he hollers, laughing.

Meanwhile, Colin keeps screaming, laughing uproariously, "Hold on to your butts, hold on to your butts!" Now the boys stand in a huddled circle, arms around shoulders, Mike and Branden, Scooter and Max, hats askew or tossed off, fingers and hands intertwined, and they are all bouncing up and down, up and down, bursting with happiness.

Sam sits transfixed in the booth. He thinks of dozens of things he could say into the microphone, but it is all there on the field. He decides in the end that silence is best. Anyone with eyes can see what's happening. Words would only spoil it.

Coach Reid watches the boys as they celebrate, resists the urge to join them, to leap arms outstretched on top of the pile. No, this is their moment. It isn't about Coach Reid, or any other adults. It is enough, *more* than enough, to stand back and watch.

Branden runs up, ecstatic. "We did it, Dad!" he exclaims. "We did it!"

The son throws his arms around the father, and the father squeezes back, hard, hoping to capture the memory like a summer firefly in his hands, wanting the moment to last for-ever, burning brightly, and knowing that somehow, amazingly, as sure as they stood, it would.

Postgame

Up in the booth, Sam Reiser clicks off the microphone. There's nothing left to say.

The game had written all the words, and now the game has gone silent.

Sam closes the scorebook, tucks the pencil into the spiral binding, stretches his arms, yawns.

His eyes drift from the happy revelers to the dejected Northeast team. To his surprise, Sam sympathizes most with Nick Clemente, bat still in his hands, still waiting on deck. The star player still yearning for one final chance to win the game.

Sam knows how he feels.

If only . . . if only . . .

The teams line up to shake hands. Parents spill onto the field. A trophy is awarded, photographs taken, videos recorded. The winners smile, the losers split.

All the while, Sam watches. Alone in the booth. Never moving from his seat. It is all he can do. The primary object in baseball is to go home, to circle the bases and return to where you began, touching that white dish, home plate. And right now, that's all Sam wants. To return home, sweet home. He yawns again, so much bad medicine in his body. He feels tired and hungry.

He brushes a strand of hair from the countertop. Sam finds hair on his pillow every morning, first in clumps, now less and less. Soon it will all be gone.

He hears the door swing open downstairs, the clattery sound of a wheelchair unfolding, then the heavy approach of footsteps. Unmistakably his father's.

"Some game, huh?" Mr. Reiser says.

"Yep," Sam replies.

There is an awkward silence between them.

It is often hard to say the right thing. What are the words? How does one express the rumblings of the heart? There's no scorecard to consult for guidance. No lineup to read. No statistics to memorize. Both the father and the son search for them, the lost elusive words, but find only silence.

"You ready?" Mr. Reiser finally asks.

Sam nods, casts his eyes to the floor.

He hates this.

The day has sucked the energy out of him. All Sam wants now is to lie on the couch under one of his grandma's hand-knit blankets, snack on something, stare at anything on TV.

"Most everybody's gone," Mr. Reiser reassures his son. "Mike is waiting downstairs."

Sam nods. Mike. The very thought exhausts him. But there's nothing to be done. It's time to go.

Sam's father is a large, barrel-chested man. Full around the middle, with sturdy legs. He bends down and grasps Sam with two strong arms. Sam's hands reflexively reach around his father's neck, as they have done many times over the past eight weeks; the left hand clasps the right wrist and holds.

Up the father lifts, up Sam rises into his father's arms, legs dangling.

The father exhales once, blows the air out in a quick burst; his legs steady, his back straightens. *Whew.*

He carries Sam down the stairs. Carefully sets his boy into the chair.

Wheels him out.

Into the light of day, into the afternoon warmth, into a world where everyone walks or runs or hops or skips.

A world where Sam rolls on two fat wheels. The sick kid with cancer. That lousy word: osteosarcoma.

Sam says, "Let's get out of here."

But up steps Mike with that look in his eyes. Mike won't let Sam be.

"Hey."

"Hey," Sam replies in a quiet voice. "You won."

Mike grins, his face shining.

Mr. Reiser coughs. "I need a Coke or something. You guys want anything?" Before they even reply, he hustles off toward the concession stand.

Mike and Sam are alone. Sam in a wheelchair. Mike at his side. "So, um, I know you said no when I asked before," Mike begins. "But I really, really don't want to go with my parents to my sister's game. Not after today."

Sam looks away. "I'm beat," he says softly. "I need to rest. There must be somebody else."

Mike takes a half step back. "There isn't anyone else, Sam," he blurts. "There's just you."

Sam hears the catch in Mike's throat. The raw emotion beneath the words. It frightens him. All this time, Sam hadn't seen it. Mike had been coming over, visiting, watching TV, playing board games, and Sam thought it was all for him. Mike visiting the sick friend. Feeling sorry for the kid with cancer.

But it was just the opposite. Mike was the one who needed something. He finally said it out loud.

Mike needed his friend back.

"I'm sorry," Sam says.

"I know," Mike answers.

"It's been so hard," Sam confesses. He swallows hard.

Mike nods, he knows.

"Well, I guess it would be okay if you came over for a little while," Sam says.

"You sure? You're not too tired?"

142

"Come on," Sam says. "You know how to steer this thing? Give me a push."

Mr. Reiser catches up with the boys at the car. He gently loads Sam into the backseat, legs stretched out. Mike sits up front.

Sam is asleep by the time they pull into the driveway. But it's okay. Mike is invited to stay anyway. He eats a late lunch with Sam's parents. Grilled cheese and milk. Sam's mom bakes brownies. Mike gets to lick the bowl. They talk about a lot of things, the game, how great it was, and about Sam, and friendship, and things that are so much harder than any boy's game.

And when Sam awakes from his nap, Mike is still there.

Acknowledgments

This book does not get written without Jean Feiwel's support, encouragement, faith, and friendship. And it does not get realized in its present form without Liz Szabla's editorial insight, direction, and care—her gentle and steady *push*.

Special thanks to Dr. Jennifer Pearce of Albany Medical Hospital, for her interest in this project, for the work she does in pediatric oncology, and for the singular debt our family owes.

Michael Geus helped immeasurably throughout the process, from swapping e-mails over the initial idea to commenting on drafts. Every writer should have a sympathetic reader; I'm grateful that mine was so bright and so kind.

Thanks to many folks at Tri-Village Little League in Delmar, New York. The players, of course, informed this book throughout. In particular, I've been fortunate to serve as a Little League coach under three able managers before taking the job myself: Reid Sperber, John Lanchantin, and the always-colorful Pete Bukowski. There's surely some small piece of each of them in these pages. I'm grateful not only for their baseball knowledge, but for the way they give of themselves to the community, good fathers all. In a time when youth coaches are routinely criticized, it's important to recognize the good work—the time and dedication—that the overwhelming majority of volunteers perform for our children.

A special shout-out to Game Six of the 1986 NLCS between the New York Mets and the Houston Astros. Just for fun, I mixed and matched the Mets' top-of-the-9th, three-run rally with the Astros' bottom-of-the-16th to create this book's final frame. And a cheer for Game Six of the 1975 World Series between the Cincinnati Reds and the Boston Red Sox. I lifted Bernie Carbo's dramatic home run from that game. Readers will find it reimagined in chapter eight of this book. A tip of the cap to the folks at Retrosheet.com for making the research so enjoyable.

When I was in the early stages of this book, puzzling over the character of Uncle Jimmy, Elliott Shaw invited me into his home to visit his "gallery," a room set aside for his personal collection of baseball memorabilia.

My appreciation goes out to more baseball writers than I can adequately list, for inhabiting and extending the great

American tradition of baseball writing. It is a dream come true to join your ranks with this modest contribution.

Much of the first draft of this book was written by hand in a spiral notebook in the Bethlehem Public Library in Delmar, New York.

And finally a "standing O" for my mother, who passed on to me the love of the game. We've watched a lot of baseball together, often in a state of high anxiety. She is forever linked in my heart with baseball, hardwired to the point where there is hardly one without the other. And that is why I love the game as I do.

None of this counts in the standings, of course, without the love of my home team: Maggie, Gavin, Nicholas, and, batting cleanup, my wife, Lisa, who is always good in the clutch.—J.P.

GOFISH

JAMES PRELLER

What did you want to be when you grew up?
As a southpaw from Long Island, I dreamed of pitching for the New York Mets.

When did you realize you wanted to be a writer?
College, at Oneonta, New York. But in my teen years, I often wrote and kept a journal. I've found that it often helps to write things down, get words on a page, to discover what I'm truly thinking and feeling. We not only write what we know, we discover what we know . . . by writing.

What's your first childhood memory?
I vividly recall hiding under a table—and refusing to come out—when my grandmother visited from Queens Village. She was old and wrinkly, with pointy glasses, and wore a dead fox around her neck. Terrifying.

What's your favorite childhood memory?
I'm the youngest of seven children, so what I remember best—outside of the manic joy of Christmas—was the chatter and clatter and spilled milk of dinnertime together. It was like a

nightly hockey game, complete with thrown elbows, clutching, grabbing, and roughing penalties.

As a young person, who did you look up to most?
Do you mean I'm not a young person anymore? I had two older sisters, and four older brothers—each remarkable and mysterious in his own way. Neil was the resident genius, who passed on to me his love of NYC and Bob Dylan; Bill was the motorhead, working in gas stations, and always the friendliest when I was little; John played guitar and had "Popeye" muscles; Al was, and still is, the stable easygoing one. And I was the pup, lapping it all up.

What was your worst subject in school?
English. Grammar, specifically.

What was your best subject in school?
P.E. and recess.

What was your first job?
Jones Beach concessions, West End Two. Great times.

How did you celebrate publishing your first book?
Very quietly.

Where do you write your books?
I usually write at my computer, in the basement of my house. Someday I dream, like the rat in *The Tale of Despereaux*, of reaching the light, the light! For *Six Innings*, I wrote much of my first draft in longhand, at the Bethlehem Public Library in Delmar, New York.

Where do you find inspiration for your writing?

Since I usually write realistic nonfiction, I try to begin with an accurate understanding of a child's world, often by sitting in on various classrooms in my community. I have three children, ages 8, 10, and 16, so that helps me stay connected. I don't think you can examine something like "childhood" under a microscope, like a lab technician in a cold, white room. For a writer, you've got to feel it, and for whatever reason, I still remember.

When you finish a book, who reads it first?

It depends on the book. My editor, usually.

Are you a morning person or a night owl?

I'm a lunch and snacktime person. But as a father in a busy house, my strategy has been to try to outlast everyone. Then the house is mine, all mine! The older I get, the tougher that becomes.

What do you value most in your friends?

Tolerance, kindness.

Where do you go for peace and quiet?

Excuse me? Peace and quiet? What in the world are you talking about?

What makes you laugh out loud?

Will Ferrell in *Old School*.

What's your favorite song?

This changes over time. I'm a huge fan of all things Dylan, constantly rediscovering songs I thought I knew. But to name one song, this moment? Townes Van Zant's, "To Live Is to Fly." Thus the character in *Six Innings*, Dylan Van Zant.

Who is your favorite fictional character?
Atticus Finch, *To Kill a Mockingbird*. I also like Frank Bascombe
from Richard Ford's novels, Rabbit—for his flaws and failures—
from John Updike's Rabbit series, and just about everybody in
Go, Dog. Go!

What are you most afraid of?
Not being able to pay my bills.

What time of year do you like best?
Spring and autumn, the transitional seasons.

What's your favorite TV show?
New York Mets baseball.

**If you were stranded on a desert island, who would
you want for company?**
My wife and children.

If you could travel in time, where would you go?
I'm most fascinated by the late '60s. And I guess I continue to return to that period, in my way, as a writer. It feels like those core
childhood years have the deepest imprint. I'm forever going
back, digging in the dirt.

**What's the best advice you have ever received about
writing?**
Write from the heart. And . . . the day you send out a book sub-
mission, start another one. The worst thing you can do is sit
around and wait for someone else's approval. Be true to yourself, that's another one.

What do you want readers to remember about your books?
That for a time they came along with me for a ride—and that they were in good hands.

What would you do if you ever stopped writing?
Edit. Books are my life's work, and I'd love to be able to play the role of an editor, help writers realize their talents, giving them the support and the opportunity that is so hard to come by. I think many of us are capable of great things, sometimes all it takes is someone in your ear, saying, "You can do this. I believe in you." So much of life is people putting limits on you, defining you, placing you in convenient boxes. It's so great when the possibilities open up. Part of being a great editor, with few exceptions, is giving up the dream of writing for yourself. The job is to serve the work, another writer's work, and I've never been able to give that up completely. A little too selfish, perhaps.

What do you like best about yourself?
Oh dear, please, no. Unpretentiousness, I guess. I certainly hate pretentiousness in other people. Anyone with a superior attitude turns me off, completely.

What is your worst habit?
Does insomnia count? I think concentration is critical to performing well in just about anything. It's why I think all of today's talk about "multi-tasking" is malarkey. I often lack the laser-like focus that is so essential to my job.

What is your best habit?
I read a lot.

What do you consider to be your greatest accomplishment?

My life as a father.

Where in the world do you feel most at home?

Is this a trick question? At home! But outside of that, I'm always happy on a hiking trail, somewhere in nature. On trips to Ireland I've felt connected in ways I can't fathom or explain. And I love— even to this day—sitting out in centerfield during a ballgame, searching the sky for high-flying baseballs (note: I play in a men's hardball league). I think it connects me to something innocent and pure, chasing a round white ball under a blue sky. I remain a boy at heart.

What do you wish you could do better?

I wish I could throw a real good fastball. And also—and this is maybe too corny to say—but to love with true selflessness.

What would your readers be most surprised to learn about you?

That I am so ordinary, so . . . unsurprising. On school visits, especially back in my early days, I was often troubled when teachers/students put "the visiting author" up on a pedestal. I'm not comfortable with that role. So then I found the solution: My task was to show them how utterly ordinary I was, that authors are no more special than doctors or architects or any one else. I'm just another guy who works hard and does his best. That I'm . . . just like them.

Do you experience writer's block?

I don't believe in it, frankly. It's one more of those "mystical" things that writers are supposed to endure. I have a lunch pail attitude to my job, since I don't have the luxury—in time or

money—to sit around waiting for the muse to descend. I'm trying to pay the bills, you know? So I make things up. What I have
learned—and what I will concede—is that there are times when
the energy fails. (Writing, to me, requires great enthusiasm and
energy.) I realized a while back that it was usually a sign that I
was boring myself: That the story I was writing, or the specific
scene, was flawed somehow. I was on the wrong path—and
boring myself to tears. When the writing is right, I am fully engaged. When bored by my own words, I need to walk away and
rethink things. Usually it means honing in a little closer to the
rumblings of my own heart.

Why did you write *Six Innings*?

I had to write a book about baseball; it was inevitable. Baseball
has touched my life in every way that it can be touched; it's an
invisible thread that connects all the corners of my life. Most
vividly in my childhood memories, most profoundly with my
mother—watching games, playing catch, connecting through
the game. As a father, I've spent a lot of time around Little
League fields. I've coached and managed many teams. I've
watched those kids, tried to help the best I could, and always
came away convinced that I learned more than they did. It's a
world I know. But more than that, it's a world where many boys
live—passionately. Serious business. We remember those
games, those times, forever. For the book, I wanted to use baseball as a way to explore character. The friendships, the strug-
gles, the inner lives as they are revealed in thought and action
during a six-inning baseball game.

Do you use real life in your books?

Yes, all the time. My experiences, thoughts, feelings, dreams—
my life is the primary source for everything I write. Could it be
any other way? I can't imagine it. For *Six Innings*, I drew upon a

lifetime of experiences. Yet surprises still came in the process of putting words on paper. One by one, different characters stepped forward. One boy, who soon served as the book's "play-by-play man," was very sick. To be honest, it was territory I resisted visiting. A place I didn't want to go. Because it was personal, something we experienced in our own family, something still raw and heartfelt, something that was not mine to own. It was my son Nick's journey, reinvented and relocated, yes, but in every meaningful way true to the core. You learn surprising things during a time of serious illness, unexpected "gifts" arrive in many forms. Oddly, you come away enriched, the heart bursting. And when you feel something that powerfully, well, that's always a good time to write.

Why children's books?

Good question. I guess, like much in life, accident played a significant role. Out of college, knowing that I wanted to write . . . I became a waiter at Beefsteak Charlie's. A year later, I moved to Brooklyn and got a job as a junior copywriter at Scholastic, pulling down $12,500 a year, writing for the K-1 SeeSaw Book Club. My job was basically to read a ton of books and describe them to teachers and kids. It required two different voices. For teachers: "In this classic tale, H.A. Rey's mischievous monkey . . ." For students: "YIKES! That crazy monkey is in trouble again!" I met a lot of great books in that job, and the dream took hold. Anyone who works with children—or, for that matter, any parent, or anyone who has ever spent time with children—knows that kids give back. They respond, purely and directly. You get an immediate response from children that is so satisfying. Today I get fan letters that amaze me. At some point kids figure out that the book in their hands was written by a real person (not, as I once imagined, beamed down from another planet). Sometimes I'll walk into a classroom and can see it in a few sets of eyes: a reverence. I am not foolish enough to believe that they are in awe of me—I'm just a guy—but they love and respect books, and actually writing one seems like such an impossible, miraculous thing. My goal is to de-mystify the process. And in short order, after spending only a few minutes in my presence, the awe fades away. To be clear: I don't believe in the cult of celebrity, but I *am* still awed by books, still feel the wonder of stories, the life-changing power of words. I am grateful to have played a small role in that Great Conversation between reader and book.

SQUARE FISH

When you're new in town, it's hard to know who to hang out with—and who to avoid.

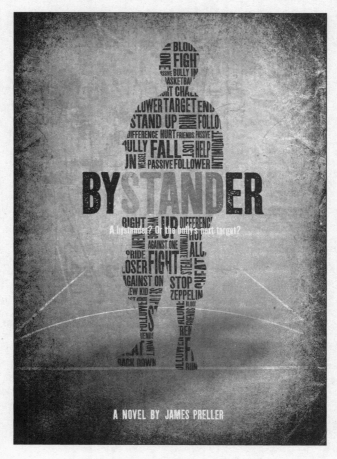

Keep reading for an excerpt from

BYSTANDER
by JAMES PRELLER

available now in hardcover from
FEIWEL AND FRIENDS.

1
[ketchup]

THE FIRST TIME ERIC HAYES EVER SAW HIM, DAVID HALLEN-
back was running, if you could call it that, running in
a halting, choppy-stepped, stumpy-legged shamble,
slowing down to look back over his shoulder, stum-
bling forward, pausing to catch his breath, then lurch-
ing forward again.

He was running *from,* not *to,* and not running, but
fleeing.

Scared witless.

Eric had never seen the boy before. But in this town,
a place called Bellport, Long Island, it was true of most

kids. Eric didn't know anybody. He bounced the basketball, flicking it with his fingertips, not looking at the ball, or the rim, or anything else on the vast, empty grounds behind the middle school except for that curly-haired kid who couldn't run to save his life. Which was too bad, really, because it looked to Eric like he might be doing exactly that—running for his life.

Eric took a halfhearted jumper, missed. No lift in his legs. The ball bounced to the left wing, off the asphalt court and onto the grass, where it rolled and settled, unchased. Eric had been shooting for almost an hour. Working on his game or just killing time, Eric wasn't sure. He was tired and hot and a little bored or else he would have bounded after the ball like a pup, pounced on it after the first bounce, spun on spindly legs, and fired up a follow-up shot. Instead he let the ball roll to the grass and, hands on his hips, dripping sweat, watched the running boy as he continued across the great lawn in his direction.

He doesn't see me, Eric thought.

Behind him there was the sprawling Final Rest Pet Cemetery. According to Eric's mother, it was supposedly the third-largest pet cemetery in the United States.

And it's not like Eric's mom was making that up just to make Eric feel better about "the big move" from Ohio to Long Island. Because, duh, nobody is going to get all pumped up just because there's a big cemetery in your new hometown, stuffed with dead cats and dogs and whatever else people want to bury. Were there pet lizards, tucked into little felt-lined coffins? Vietnamese potbellied pigs? Parakeets? People were funny about pets. But burying them in a real cemetery, complete with engraved tombstones? That was a new one on Eric. A little *excessive*, he thought.

As the boy drew closer, Eric could see that his shirt was torn. Ripped along the side seam, so that it flapped as he ran. And . . . was that blood? There were dark red splotches on the boy's shirt and jeans (crazy to wear those on a hot August afternoon). Maybe it was just paint. The whole scene didn't look right, that much was sure. No one seemed to be chasing after the boy. He had come from the far side of the school and now traveled across the back of it. The boy's eyes kept returning to the corner of the building, now one hundred yards away. Nothing there. No monsters, no goblins, no ghosts, no *thing* at all.

Eric walked to his basketball, picked it up, tucked it under his arm, and stood watching the boy. He still hadn't spotted Eric, even though he was headed in Eric's direction.

At last, Eric spoke up. "You okay?" he asked. Eric's voice was soft, even gentle, but his words stopped the boy like a cannon shot to the chest. He came to a halt and stared at Eric. The boy's face was pale, freckled, mushy, with small, deep-set eyes and a fat lower lip that hung like a tire tube. He looked distrustful, a dog that had been hit by too many rolled-up newspapers.

Eric stepped forward, gestured to the boy's shirt. "Is that blood?"

The boy's face was blank, unresponsive. He didn't seem to understand.

"On your shirt," Eric pointed out.

The boy looked down, and when his eyes again lifted to meet Eric's, they seemed distant and cheerless. There was a flash of something else there, just a fleeting something in the boy's eyes: hatred.

Hot, dark hatred.

"No, no. Not . . . bl-blood," the boy said. There might have been a trace of a stutter in his voice, something in the way he paused over the "bl" consonant blend.

Whatever it was, the red glop was splattered all over the boy's pants and shirt. Eric could see traces of it in the boy's hair. Then Eric smelled it, a familiar whiff, and he knew. Ketchup. The boy was covered with ketchup.

Eric took another step. A look of panic filled the boy's eyes. He tensed, stepped back, swiveled his head to again check the far corner of the building. Then he took off without a word. He moved past Eric, beyond the court, through a gap in the fence, and into the cemetery.

"Hey!" Eric called after him. "I'm not—"

But the ketchup boy was long gone.

IF YOU LIKE SPORTS,
you'll love these SQUARE FISH sports books!

Airball • L. D. Harkrader
ISBN: 978-0-312-37382-5
$6.99 US /$7.99 Can

If you want to play on this team,
you've got to do it in your underwear.

Funerals and Fly Fishing • Mary Bartek
ISBN: 978-0-312-56124-6
$6.99 US / $8.99 Can

Open caskets, dead bodies, and a bag of
scalps—Brad is in for a creepy summer.

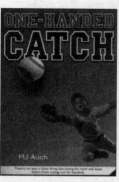

One-Handed Catch • MJ Auch
ISBN: 978-0-312-53575-9
$6.99 US / $8.99 Can

Not even losing his hand will keep
Norm from trying out for the
baseball team.

Six Innings • James Preller
ISBN: 978-0-312-60240-6
$6.99 US / $8.50 Can

It's the biggest game of the season,
but Sam Reiser has to sit it out.

Top of the Order • John Coy
ISBN: 978-0-312-61111-8
$6.99 US / $8.50 Can

Four sports-crazy boys deal with
family, school, and friendship during
baseball season.

SQUARE FISH
WWW.SQUAREFISHBOOKS.COM
AVAILABLE WHEREVER BOOKS ARE SOLD

ALSO AVAILABLE
FROM SQUARE FISH BOOKS
FIVE DIFFERENT BOYS—FIVE WAYS TO NEVER GIVE UP

Alabama Moon • Watt Key
ISBN: 978-0-312-64480-2
$6.99 US / $8.50 Can

NOW A MAJOR MOTION PICTURE!
The touching story of a boy who must
find a way to survive on his own after
losing his father.

Home of the Brave • Katherine Applegate
ISBN: 978-0-312-53563-6
$6.99 US / $7.99 Can

A beautifully wrought novel about a
journey from hardship to hope.

★ "Moving . . . representative of all
immigrants."—*School Library Journal*,
Starred Review

Junebug • Alice Mead
ISBN: 978-0-312-56126-0
$6.99 US / $8.99 Can

A boy. A birthday. A dream of a
better life far, far away.

"Readers will be rooting for Junebug
and his dreams all the way."
—*Kirkus Reviews*

Wing Nut • MJ Auch
ISBN: 978-0-312-38420-3
$6.99 US / $7.99 Can

Sometimes "home" is found where
you least expect it.

"A good book for reluctant boy
readers."—*Booklist*

Defiance • Valerie Hobbs
ISBN: 978-0-312-53581-0
$7.99 US / $10.25 Can

Eleven-year-old Toby Steiner, battling cancer,
finds inspiration from an old woman and
strength from a broken-down cow.

★ "Real and poignant."
—*Kirkus Reviews*, Starred Review

SQUARE FISH
WWW.SQUAREFISHBOOKS.COM
AVAILABLE WHEREVER BOOKS ARE SOLD